Sometimes destiny can

M000290168

CONSTANT GRAY

RYAN TAYLOR

FBI Anti-Piracy Warning: The unauthorized reproduction or distribution of a copyrighted work is illegal. Criminal copyright infringement, including infringement without monetary gain, is investigated by the FBI and is punishable by up to five years in federal prison and a fine of $250,000.

Advertencia Antipirateria del FBI: La reproducción o distribución no autorizada de una obra protegida por derechos de autor es ilegal. La infracción criminal de los derechos de autor, incluyendo la infracción sin lucro monetario, es investigada por el FBI y es castigable con pena de hasta cinco años en prisión federal y una multa de $250,000.

Constant Gray

First Edition

Copyright © 2018 Ryan Taylor

ISBN-13: 978-1-947392-11-3

All rights reserved. No part of this book may be used or reproduced in any manner whatsoever, including Internet usage, without written permission from the author.

This story is a work of fiction. References to real people, events, establishments, organizations, or locales are intended only to provide a sense of authenticity and are used fictitiously. All other characters, and all incidents and dialogue are drawn from the author's imagination and are not to be construed as real.

Cover design by Damonza.com

Book formatted by Damonza.com

For Ari, Emma, Lyric, and Elektra
"Always seek to find your balance in this world."

"Be careful when you cast out your demons that you don't throw away the best of yourself."

-Friedrich Nietzsche

Equilibrium can only be maintained by moving forward. The scale is tipped in this world, and it has festered for too long. Humanity needs a hero. I don't know it yet, but I am the hand that will bring balance.

CHAPTER 1
DRIP, DRIP, DRIP

DRIP

    Drip

    Drip

    Drip

    Drip

    Drip

    The cadence sang in my ears.

    My heart and my head pulsed simultaneously with each drip.

    The same pattern had occurred for months. Every two to three seconds.

Drip.

    You'd think it would have driven me crazy, maybe it did. Fuck if I knew. I'd been tied up down in this place for months. I couldn't even recall how I got here. Every time I got a thought or caught a glimpse of something.

Drip.

    Back to square one again.

    The stench in the room reeked a putrid odor. A mix of rust, copper, and month-old chicken someone left to sour in the fridge. I was glad they'd blindfolded me, or else I might have known what really made that awful smell.

I imagined the rust scent came from the water that had been dripping for months, the copper possibly a pipe, and the chicken smell? It might have been chicken. Let's just say I'm optimistic. Not sure why, but hell I tried to be.

Aside from the incessant dripping, a door upstairs constantly opened and closed. It was inconsistent in its timing though. It wasn't mechanical, probably people going in and out of a door, or wind shifting through it.

God knows I could have used some fresh air. At one point, a good breeze from the air conditioning blew through, but whoever brought me here originally must have decided to either stop paying their bill, or just kept it running exclusively upstairs.

I thought it had been months, but I couldn't recall the last time I heard another person in this room. At one point, it seemed fairly busy. People touched me all over my body.

They would lift my legs, move my feet, or rotate my jaw back and forth. I wasn't sure what they wanted really, I just did what any good prisoner would do. I took it and didn't offer any complaints.

Even when they cut me open at times. I took the pain and laid quietly. I thought by being "good," they might have decided to let me go. Turned out it to be the opposite; I seemed to be the head of the class.

I used to hear other people like me down here moaning and screaming in pain. They would all get shuffled out and removed after they'd been used up. I just always had stamina I guess. As far as I could remember back anyways.

I'm not sure what kept me going, but I imagined that I had someone out there important to me that I needed to see. Could have been a dog, or maybe a cat? Nah, probably not a cat. I was definitely a dog person. I bet I had an English bulldog with a squished-up face. I'd have called him Rupert.

I thought a lot when my mind drifted off. Around here, one didn't have the luxury to just get up and dance if he got bored.

Here I lied, chained to a gurney, blind folded, and gagged. It seemed rather dull, if you weren't into that sort of thing.

Drip

Drip

Drip

"Hello?" Came a sound from upstairs.

I tried to open my eyes, but realized once again the blindfold impeded my vision, and the gag prevented me from answering them. How easily you get used to it.

I sat quietly and acted like a good prisoner.

"Hello?!" I heard it again, a man's voice echoing out. Big too from the way his voice thundered and bounced off the walls and pipes. Not that a man's voice can be indicative of his size, probably a bit presumptuous on my part.

I heard some loud crashes upstairs, things were being moved around. My body prickled from the cold as I listened.

"There's no one here. This place must have been abandoned years ago." I heard someone say through the ceiling.

"Yeah, I bet we could set up in here and no one would even notice." The original voice said.

That couldn't be true. I'd only been down here a few months, right?

The pipes groaned, shaking violently from lack of use over the years. The whole building seemed to shake.

"Plumbing works and the water is flowing!" a female voice shouted out.

I heard more things scraping against the floor upstairs, it sounded like music to me. Something I had not heard in forever. I enjoyed every little strange noise.

Metal grated against the concrete. Someone dragged a table

across the floor. The people talked to one another. I clung to every syllable like it would be my last.

"Dude, this place is grumble. There's junk everywhere, and it smells like a fucking sewer." The deep voice rumbled.

"Shut up Reese, this place is amazing! How many places have we been able to squat at that had water?" the female said.

"She's right, just one," answered the third voice.

Two males and one female. How wonderful, it had been too long.

So refreshing to have company after all this time. However long it had been, I forgot.

"What the hell is that?" said the female voice.

"I don't know, it looks like a refrigerator," the third voice answered.

"No shit Sherlock, I know it's a fucking fridge, what is that behind it?" she retorted.

Scraping and grunting came from up the stairs. The voices seemed to be getting louder.

"Whoa," the female said.

"Dude, this is some horror film shit," the third voice said.

"It's a door," Reese said. "Should I open it?" he asked.

"Hell yeah," the girl said.

"You are way too eager to get chopped up and eaten Maddy," said the third one.

"Well, being a horror movie, they always kill the black guy first Anthony." She laughed loudly.

The door bucked and shook, the walls quaked as well. Debris and dust fell from the ceiling and landed on my body. My guess about his size seemed to hold merit now. Reese had great strength.

All the muscles in the world would not budge that door though. It couldn't have been more than a few weeks old; I'd overheard them saying they were putting it up due to smells wafting outside the basement. The guy who cut us up complained about it often, he had a thick southern accent. So, I doubt they woul-

BOOM! BOOM! BOOM!

SNAP! POP!

Creeeeaaaaaaaaakkkkkkkk. The door protested loudly.

Silence again, then a fit of coughing broke out from the party upstairs.

"Holy shit, I think I'm going to puke," groaned Anthony.

"Ugh, me too," Maddy said. I could hear her rush across the room upstairs.

I heard footsteps thumping down the stairs. It had been months since I'd heard that. In a few moments, I would be examined and cut open again.

Click-Click I heard the light switch being tested.

"Hmm," Reese said.

"Any axe murderers down there?" Maddy chimed in, "If so, tell em' we got a black guy up here!" She laughed again.

Anthony sighed.

"So long as I keep my shirt on, no one will kill me." She laughed.

"Then you are better than dead. You can't keep your top on, much less your legs closed," Anthony said laughing.

"Fuck you," she snapped.

The footsteps glided cautiously through the room. There were several breaks in the cadence of his steps. He must have stopped and examined something. His breathing slowed down.

"Well?! What the hell is down there?" Maddy yelled out from the doorway up the stairs.

"Stay upstairs," he said evenly.

I felt the warmth of a body next to my left arm. This is how the process always started, he would begin by feeling my body all over. I would be thoroughly examined, and they would decide what they wanted to take.

"Holy shit," Reese said right next to me. I felt the air from his voice brush against my skin. Goosebumps rippled across my skin.

"You're alive," he said.

"Who's alive?" Anthony said as he tromped down the stairs. I heard him gasp.

"What the fuck?! Let's get the fuck out of here. This is some dark arts shit." Anthony continued. "Seriously Reese, we don't want to be messing with these people or their shit. Reese..." he implored.

Reese's breathing never changed, he had the same steady breath the whole time.

I felt a hand on my shoulder. A large bear sized hand, just as I had suspected. Calloused fingers from a hard life sat idle before I felt my right arm being lifted from the table. I heard the chains clank off the side of the gurney. They were choosing the things they wanted, this is what they always did, this was the process.

He reached over and did the same thing to my right leg. The chains made a ringing noise off the table again. Funny, I could barely feel the weight of my own leg. The pressure of his hand the only thing I could feel. Kind of like when you sit down on the toilet too long and your legs go numb. I felt needles as the blood flowed into my legs. Lastly, I felt his hands on my face. The tips of his fingers running along my temples and cheekbones. The same numbness throughout. Slight pressure from his fingers around the back of my head, I felt his fingers wrap around the straps that held the gag in place, they submitted to Reese's strength as they snapped off.

Stagnant air poured into my lungs, I breathed in deeply. The air refreshed me, I did not taste the rotten air like I thought I would have. I reveled in its sweetness, utterly euphoric after so long.

I guess it's like they said about not knowing you stunk, because you were around it and got used to it. Only fresh air here. So good to salivate again. You never know how much you'll miss something until you're a prisoner of people harvesting your body parts.

"Are you ok?" Reese asked me.

"Sure boss," My vocal chords rattled the dust off after such a lack of use, my words came out more gravelly than I was used to.

"How long have you been down here?" he asked.

"Dude, are you really fucking talking to a corpse? Did he just talk?!" Anthony asked. "What the fuck is going on down there?" Maddy yelled.

"Nothing!" Reese's powerful voice boomed. "Stay upstairs!"

Reese must have turned to Anthony because his voice shifted. "Get upstairs, don't tell her shit. We have to let this guy go," he said.

Me? Was he going to let me go?

Anthony must have gotten the message, because I heard him run back up the stairs.

I felt huge fingers on my face, the light hit me as the mask came off. The change in pressure on my face was a welcome respite. I blinked away the spots in my vision as my eyes adjusted. I saw Reese standing there as he looked at me.

A tall, handsome kid stood in front of me. Probably in his mid-twenties. His scruffy blond beard and shaggy blond hair were covered in dust. His pallid blue eyes, with deep blue ridges throughout them like when you drop a rock into water, opened wide in what I interpreted as curiosity.

I felt the blood flowing through my body again, like small spiders running up and down my arms and legs, every foot making its pressure felt. My muscles slowly worked themselves back to life. I flexed my hands and felt each nerve still intact.

"Am I free to go now? Have I met all the needs you require?" I asked Reese.

His brow creased in confusion. He shook his head sideways.

"Look, just lie there and I'll try to find a key or a hammer or something."

I lied there, closed my eyes, and listened to where he went.

"There is a desk in the corner to your left, it has five drawers." I said to him.

"Ok I see it," he said.

"Open the top drawer."

Clang Clang the drawer was locked.

"It's lo—"

"Hit it with your right hand on the top, near the right side of the drawer," I told him.

Pop I heard the lock disengage.

"Try now," I said.

I heard the drawer slide open.

"Wow, that's some memory you have," he said.

"Check the third drawer, there is a false panel that the keys are hidden in."

The drawer creaked like it always did, I heard him fumbling around the drawer until it popped. Then the sound of keys jingling.

"Which one?" he asked.

"Run your fingers over them," I said.

He ran his fingers over the keys.

The key I needed had a tinny sound to it, not the heavy thunk of a cheap metal, but the light sound of silver. Though I doubted they had a silver key.

His finger made purchase with the key. I opened my eyes.

"That one," I said.

He grabbed it and brought it over.

"I don't know how you did that, but color me fucking impressed," he rumbled.

He went from arm to arm, and then from leg to leg with the keys, deftly unlocking each one.

My muscles had all their flow back by now. I sat up and

looked around the room that had been my prison. The walls were covered in occultist markings, pentagrams, blood, possibly shit. Pools of gore and other dry liquids lay congealed on the floor. Large white coolers sat all around the room and along each wall. I wasn't sure of the contents, but I imagined an organic material. Seemed like somewhere that they might have put our parts to keep them preserved.

"So, are you ok? I mean you look healthy enough," Reese said eyeing me over.

I sat nude on the gurney, my legs hanging off the edge. I looked at my body, I did in fact look healthy. My skin was soft with dimpled red marks from where the chains had barred my escape. My black hair hung to my shoulders at this point, I hated it this long. This beard had forgone my normal limits for it as well.

Still tan after all this time in a basement too. My muscles were in good shape too, I flexed and felt strength within my stagnant body. I should have been emaciated.

I couldn't remember the last time I'd actually eaten, or had anything to drink for that matter. It couldn't have been more than a month though, I always heard people could not live that long without water.

I do remember being cut open and having parts removed. Yet I didn't see anything missing, not a single scar on my body. I had all ten fingers and ten toes. Had I dreamt all those surgeries? Fuck if I knew.

This was not exactly a normal standard for anyone. I looked up at Reese, remembering his question. *Was I ok?*

"I guess so," I said. "Thanks for letting me go."

I leaned to my left. A stainless-steel tray sat next to the gurney. A good choice for a medical tray, easy to clean I bet. I picked it up and whipped Reese in the neck as hard as I could.

He never saw it coming. A satisfying crack echoed off the

walls. His body dropped limp to the floor. I leaned down to his body and undressed him.

I calmly put his clothes on. His frame was much broader than mine, so the clothes hung loosely all over me. It was alright though. I hated being nude.

Anthony ran down the stairs at the noise. Reese probably should have listened to him.

"What the fuck man?" Anthony rushed down and looked at me standing in his dead friend's clothing. Eyes wide and his jaw agape.

"I guess in the horror movies the big guy dies first?" I asked him with a shrug.

"Fuck you man!" He reached into his star covered backpack. I stood and watched him pull out a gun. Not a model I knew, something simple though. A revolver. They were all the same though. Clunky and unreliable.

He cocked the hammer back, and I listened intently.

"It's empty," I said to him.

His eyes grew wider, sweat dripped down his temple. "How the hell did you know that?"

I charged at him with the tray and hit him in the leg, his shin splintered neatly. The large gun fell to the ground and split the tile. Anthony looked up at me, defeat in his eyes.

"Come on man! He was trying to—"

His skull caved under the weight of the tray. Just one sharp blow. His head lulled to one side as he toppled over.

I watched him slump over and stop breathing before I strolled over to where his gun fell on the ground and took it. Leaning down to his body, seeing as he was so small, I checked his pockets because the clothes were no good to me.

His wallet only contained three dollar bills. No ID, no Smith's card, nothing. I took the wallet and shoved it in my back pocket. Glancing up the stairs, I saw cigarette smoke wafting down. It smelled amazing. I must have had a kick with cigarettes in the past that I couldn't recall. My mouth watered for a smoke.

I walked upstairs into an empty, dust covered kitchen.

A thick coating of filth covered the walls and mold crept through cracks in the grout of the countertop tile. The floor was covered in grease and the filthy white refrigerator lay on its side.

It looked like the place had been abandoned for years, much less a few months. No sign of any kind of traffic here. The grease on the floor lay thick aside from the few smudges where the kids stomped through it. The scent of cigarette smoke urged me onward. "Maddy?" I asked out loud.

Someone shuffled quietly in the other room. I turned my attention and snuck up to the opening. There were some swinging doors that clung desperately to their hinges. I pushed them and watched as they creaked and careened into one another with loud whacks. I smiled widely, that's one mystery solved.

They were doors to a kitchen. Where the waiters and the staff had undoubtedly passed back and forth through them. I had spent my time locked away in what used to be a restaurant. Just some forgotten shithole for passersby to seek respite within.

I swung the dilapidated doors open and saw a neglected dining room. Tables and chairs littered the floors, many lying on their sides. A few green pleather booths sat covered in dust and dirt. The front window read something backwards, words that had faded long ago.

A simple place, with meager decorations. Paintings of plains and fields littered the walls. Cowboy stuff mostly, and a clock that had stopped working rested on the wall. It read 1:43. Well, I know that even a broken clock is right at least twice a day, or so the cliché went.

A young woman rocking a freshly shaved head lounged in one of the remaining booths smoking a cigarette. She looked up and saw me. Her piercing emerald green eyes met mine before I took in her ruby lips. I could see from the prints left on her cigarette, she was wearing thick lipstick. "So?" She asked in a raspy voice. Smoke escaped slowly from her mouth and nose. "Who the fuck are you supposed to be?"

"Reese," I said as I motioned to my new clothes. "May I have a cigarette?"

Eyeing me up and down cautiously, she opened her pack of reds and pulled out a lone cigarette. Her earrings glinted from the sun as she turned her head.

"You going to kill me too?" She raised an eyebrow as she handed me the cigarette.

I took it from her hand, and put it between my lips. Even unlit, it tasted fantastic. She lit the tip for me. A butane lighter. Fuck I hated the smell of butane, it gave me a headache. I winced. She nodded in agreement as she took in the look on my face.

"I hate the smell too." She waved the lighter in her hand. "It gives me a headache, but its far more reliable than matches."

Half of my face curled up into a half smile, and I sat down on the other side of the booth. A cloud of dust wafted skyward as I did this. I swept aside some of the dust and rubble covering the bench. It clattered lightly to the floor.

It didn't feel like I had been a prisoner for months, or years. I felt fresh, like I'd just woken up from a good nap. Not one of those naps that went for too long that left you feeling like shit, but a nice half hour nap that fixed you right up again. It seemed surreal. I could still be dreaming right now, but this cigarette tasted too damn good, and far too satisfying for me to believe that.

After she inhaled deeply, Maddy spoke again.

"Why did you kill them?" She pointed towards the kitchen with her lipstick covered cigarette. Smoke poured from her nostrils.

"They were more than they seemed," I lifted my shoulders in a dismissive shrug.

She tilted her head sideways at me.

"What do you mean? Like they were creepers or something?" She thumped her cigarette to knock the ash off onto the floor.

I thought about this for a second.

"No, not creepers, their souls emanated a black circle. Several, in fact. This means they committed awful sins."

She cocked her eyebrow at me again.

"That's fucked. Are you some kind of priest?" She asked after taking another drag on the cigarette. The cherry on her cigarette lit her face up brightly in the dark room. The bridge of her nose had light freckles scattered across it.

"No. I just act on instinct. Auras hide no secrets."

"And being able to judge someone from seeing their "Aura?" She motioned quotation marks with her fingers. "What does mine have?"

I looked at her and studied her aura briefly.

"It's orange. It means you have good within." I said as I thumped ash onto the table.

"Ha!" She snorted. "Fuck me, that's great! Guess those people I've killed will feel better now that I have a fucking orange aura!" She sniffed and rubbed the heel of her right hand over her scalp.

I took a long drag on my cigarette. The smoke burned my lungs, but gave me a release I imagined I hadn't had in years. This place was quiet, except for Maddy and I. I could only hear the strong winds blowing outside.

"Just means you killed the right people," I said with an upward glance at her.

I put the rest of my cigarette out on the table, and got up from my seat. I looked at Maddy as I knocked the dust from my newly acquired shorts. "Keep the faith," I said to her.

She laughed and tossed me the rest of her cigarettes.

"You clearly need these more than me. Be seeing you around," she snickered.

"One last thing," I said.

"Shoot." She leaned back against the booth and put her cigarette out on the table top.

"What's the date today?"

She pulled out something from her small purse. It looked like a calendar, she flipped a few pages. "October 2nd, 2029." She looked up at me.

I don't know when I got captured, but I did know I had been here for years now. Not months.

CHAPTER 2

THE NEW WORLD

THE LIGHT BLINDED me. Stark white, like turning on a television in a pitch-black room. I couldn't blink away the blind spots in my eyes. The wind blew fiercely, it kicked dust into the lining of my clothing, making me uncomfortable immediately. I turned and observed the surroundings and saw that everything stood sun-bleached. Street and store signs that might have once said something clearly, were faded with remnants of color from the past.

The buildings themselves were mostly wreckage. Scattered remains from buildings tumbled aimlessly. Glass from shattered windows that might have littered the ground, had long since blown away. The few buildings around the area hummed various melodies from the wind that blew through their empty windows.

I took a deep breath and held it for a beat. The air smelled clear, with a slight hint of sulfur to it. An odd odor for sure, like the smell of fireworks. Typically, a smell of bad omens.

I heard the door behind me slam loudly and saw Maddy standing there with a tattered crimson scarf whipping over her face. Her short-upturned nose and high cheekbones hidden. Thick black glasses covered the rest of her pretty face. I got the feeling she was staring at me behind those lenses, questioning my intentions.

"So, you got somewhere in mind?" she asked me as she strode over.

I pondered this as I looked at her. I turned back at the torrid landscape in front of me. "I'm going this way." I pointed to the west where several street signs bucked wildly in the wind. "It looks like a freeway."

"Why?" she asked plainly.

"Instincts," I said.

"Welllll, I think that's righteous and all, but I'd suggest the opposite direction since that way…"

I had already set off before she could finish her sentence.

I walked for almost a mile. The wind ripped at my skin, forcing my oversized clothing to slap back and forth. I would have to replace these clothes soon, they were a nuisance. I wasn't a surfer, I was a—.

What was I? Who was I? I stood still for a second and stared into the glaring sun. The gigantic orb stood solid white and didn't seem to have budged since I first stepped outside the diner.

While I stared up at the sun, I heard the crunch of boots in the sand. Turning, I spotted a man who was six-foot-tall and of comparable size a few yards away. He stood draped in black leather. The movie Mad Max flashed through my mind. He wore goggles, a black mask, and a cliché black leather jacket, buttoned up the front with some makeshift spiked shoulders. The spiked club on his hip swayed back and forth in the wind. He stared intently at me. I needed to expedite the process here. I still had a lot to catch up on.

"Do you plan on staring all day, or do you actually have something vital to tell me?" I asked him pointedly.

He simply turned his left shoulder to show me a red sigil of a horned skull with an eye in its open mouth. He pointed at it with his thumb, and motioned to me as if I was going to have the slightest fucking clue as to what it could be. It looked like a band patch."Oh, you like metal?" I nodded. "Good stuff!" I raised my eyebrows and motioned with a single hand thumb up and a grin.

He reached to his waist and grabbed his club with his right hand. *What the fuck?* He didn't have a horrible aura, even though it did have a few stains on it.

Murder and abuse. I'd seen much worse earlier on Reese and Anthony. This dude's stains were old and partially faded. See, recent sins were bold black things, pitch in color, often blotting out most of the aura.Oh well, none of this was going to matter in a few seconds.

"I guess this works out. I do like your leather." I said as he walked towards me with the makeshift cudgel.

There's a moment of Zen that I loved about fighting. Right before everything began, the anticipation was thrilling, and I knew I would feel great after this. I didn't know how I would fair at this point since I'd been locked away for some years now. I was going to soak it up though. I watched him and stood still until the very last moment possible.

He jogged up to me with squinted eyes and a sneer, the club gripped in his gloved hands. They were covered in dust and well worn, with several cracks in them right around the knuckles. The club looked like the end of a pool cue with nails driven into it. A strange device for aggression, but it's possible there wasn't much else for him to use at this point.

His jog turned into a full sprint. Dust plumed high behind him as he ran. He reared his club overhead, it left his stance wide open. I wanted to test my muscles though, so I let him inside my guard.

He swung downward with the club. I leaned back and he over-extended to my left. He cursed and tried to connect a hit with the side of my head. A brain splattering deathblow if he landed it. While he leaned back for the attack, he left his ribs vulnerable. I planted my right knee into them and placed my hands on his back for added leverage.

The crushing blow from my right knee to his ribs sent tremors through my fingertips. Cracking bones told me I still had it after all this time. I stepped back as he dropped to the ground, the club still gripped tightly in his hand.

I stood back and stared down at him. Eying his slow movements, I enjoyed the sound of his juddered breathing. I imagined his now punctured lung fighting desperately for air. He stood and clung to his ribs with his left arm while he grasped the club in his right. Leaning in, he clumsily lunged at me. No one could question his tenacity at this point, nor his stupidity. This time his swing moved slower and far less steady than before. A simple maneuver to step inside and his elbow caught me on the shoulder. I planted my right foot and shifted my body up into the hit. His elbow snapped, hyper-extending on my shoulder. The impact stung for certain, but a fair trade for the damage I dealt to him.

He reeled as he finally dropped his club. I watched him fumble with his jacket as he backed away from me. With his left hand, he produced a small gun from his jacket pocket. A fat barreled, candy apple red revolver. I thought he might try to burn a hole in my throat. Instead he pointed it upwards and fired it off. It made a *wooshing* noise and a trail of light followed it skyward. It was a flare gun. Hmm, calling for backup I surmised.

"You have got to get the fuck out of here!" I heard over the roar of the gun and the wind.

I glanced over my shoulder and saw Maddy kicking up sand as she ran my way.

The man turned begun to run.

Oh no you don't.

I snatched his club out of the sand and hurled it at his legs. End over end in the air it went. It smacked him in the back of the leg, right between his thigh and his calf. His knee buckled and he toppled forward into the dirt. I charged forward and leapt onto his back. My knee crushed deep into the nape of his neck. He stopped moving overall. Just like with Reese, I began removing his leather clothing. What I wouldn't do for a clothing store, it would make getting an outfit so much easier.

Maddy caught up to me at this point. "Look man, the damned Shavs are going to be coming soon!"

I didn't turn to her as I continued getting my opponent undressed.

"No idea what that is. I cannot fear what I do not know."

I removed the remaining clothes from the downed leather clad combatant, and donned the clothing over the top of Reese's clothing. The jacket wouldn't button up properly, I had a larger chest than this guy did, so it left the bright yellow shirt showing through the open chest. Oh well.

Next, I wiggled the burnished metal framed goggles from his face and placed them on my dust covered face. They were a welcome thing, sort of. The pressure reminded me a bit of the blindfold I wore for years.

The whole outfit change took just shy of two minutes, not bad. One problem. The clothing fit well, but it was saturated with sweat. Gross. I would deal with it in lieu of the sun though. The musty odor would pass as well. It sure as hell beat running around in the light clothing I had just removed.Oh well. My black hair whipped across my face as the wind picked up speed. I was pretty sure I hated my hair long, I wondered if I could find a barber somewhere. Yeah right. The goggles at least held some of it back.

"Look man, you got the clothes and his gear, can we bolt? They have guns and shit. Not your typical group. Faul is a maniac!" she rasped with terror in her eyes.

She ranted and I continued to not know what the hell she rambled on about. Then something occurred to me.

"You're a bit of a coward, aren't you?" I asked plainly as I searched the prone man.

"I'm a survivor you idiot." She threw her arms outwardly. "I'm only here to watch your dumb ass."

"I don't need your help. I'm fully capable of handling myself." I told this to the prone body on the ground.

"Says the guy who just got rescued from a gurney!" She laughed nervously.

She had me there.

"Fair point," I said. "Thanks for that." I added as I turned to look at her.

"Can we just leave?" she implored.

I strapped the boots on my feet. They were just the right size. That's luck for you. At six-feet tall, with size fifteen shoes, I had huge feet for my height.

He didn't happen to be wearing socks though. The no socks thing was awful. It felt like a boot full of soggy sandpaper. I would have to remedy this later though. Engines rumbled in the distance, probably on their way to eat us, or something unpleasant like that. I leaned over and grabbed the flare gun from the ground. You never knew when something would come in handy. We left the man cooking in the sun.

As we hurried along the tattered terrain, Maddy insisted on ceaselessly rambling.

"So look, here's the deal. There are thirteen gods." She motioned with her fingers. Maddy spoke with her hands, like an old televangelist might have. Everything was very grandiose with her. You could have watched her with the sound turned off and still made out what she said.

"They're all supposed to represent some old Gods, or some shit. I think the whole thing is stupid, religion in general you know. Don't get me wrong. The whole reason this planet is torn in two is because of…" She carried on talking as we walked along the roadway.

The path appeared long neglected, potholes hid in the sand just waiting to snap your ankle from a misstep. The metal barriers that lined the road were long removed, possibly to become shelter from the weather. The few signs that littered this path were in relatively good shape. They gave us a way to follow. If they survived this area, we probably could too.

The dust whipped around in spirals. Kind of funny how life echoed that sentiment. Shit would get kicked up and settled after a bit, only to be stepped on by the next disturbance. Starting the cycle anew.

Never perfect; things always changed. I strove for normality. That happy center that most people could never achieve for the mere fact they didn't think it existed. They either believed a right way or a wrong way were the only options. They were on either side of a fence.

I liked to sit in the middle and live my life my way. Whoever treaded into the waters disturbed the stillness regardless of input or side. If I got out of balance, I would change the world until it met me in the middle.

Maddy still rambled on with some story about something. I watched her fling her hands about randomly as she spoke.

"That's why the Shavs run this area and the other gangs live in the dark. Access to gas and electricity is only for the rich! Those assholes and their revolutions! Who believed there could be a happy ending to the damned apocalypse? Humans were nothing but ants under the feet of giants! No one spoke for us! They just up and left! Fucking Angels and Demons man!" She rattled on aimlessly.

I gazed upward at the white expanse. "What time does the sun go down?" I asked as I squinted at the sky.

Maddy stopped and furrowed her large eyebrows at me.

"Are you effing serious? What the hell am I over here talking about?!"

"No idea. I thought you just needed to vent." I shrugged as I walked past her.

"Christ on a bicycle." She placed her hand over her face and followed after me. "The sun doesn't go down. Not on this side of the Earth anyway. There are twelve thousand miles of light, and twelve thousand miles of dark." She rolled her eyes. "I did say that already."

"Hmm." I sniffed and blew some sand out of my nose. "Why?"

She bit her lip and pinched the bridge of her nose. Visibly annoyed. "There was a war, God turned the sun white after the devil turned the world black." She shrugged. "Gave him an edge or something."

"And all this happened when?" I asked as some paper blew by us. I watched as it spiraled away in the direction we left. We had covered some decent ground, but the sulfur smell stayed right with us.

"The last twenty years or so! Do I have to repeat myself?!"

She shook her hands in front of me.

"No. Just missed a lot. I'll catch up." I said nonchalantly and nodded my head.She rolled her eyes again. Perhaps it was a tick.

We continued along the path in front of us.

CHAPTER 3
ABYSM

THE DAY DRAGGED on endlessly, and the Shavs seemed to lag behind us for a few hours. Their engines only heard sporadically in the distance. Someone once told me that making a serpentine getaway could be the ideal way to lose someone. So, we tried it out, winding our way through the sparse buildings and landscape.

We entered a decrepit suburb, the houses were intermittently laid out. There could have been a water treatment plant here as well, because it had an ammonia smell that lingered in the air, that coupled with the sulfur made my head ache.

Some of the homes in the area still had roofs on them, we weaved our way through other people's lost lives. Pictures hung on the walls of family fun, some remained in good shape, even with this blistering sun. Nothing valuable remained in any of the homes however, they appeared to have been picked clean long ago. More than likely from the very people who followed us.

We crawled around and through the sparse cover, whatever became available to hide us worked out well. We made this effort for a few hours, and it must have worked. The sound of the engines now absent. They seemed to have stopped following us now.

As well as I could remember, I had always been more than capable at fighting, but that was no reason to saddle up against a truckload of leather clad modern-day barbarians with guns and pointy sticks. The odds were not in our favor. I felt that they would be pissed that they lost a guy, but they would more than likely get a laugh at his stupidity from losing to some dude in a yellow shirt and board shorts.

In all honesty, the man I had the scrap with was still alive, at least when I left him he was. I had made sure to only fracture a single cervical vertebra; I would guess the third or fourth. He would still be able to breath, but he wouldn't be running any marathons anytime soon.

Maddy stared at me with her thick eyebrows creased judgingly. I could tell her patience was dwindling, she was chewing her nails again. This was an unattractive trait, not that my opinion of her mattered. Compared to the current state of things, I'm sure she could be very fetching to those looking. We were surrounded by a plethora of dirt, pothole laden roads, and gangs named after ominous beings to look forward to. So ultimately, she seemed pretty spectacular.

She cocked an eyebrow when she noticed my staring.

"What the hell are you gawking at? You're not my type." She said, looking up at me with her green eyes.

I shrugged. "I was just noticing that you pick at yourself a lot. You have a lot of tics."

She spat something out of her mouth onto the floor.

"Like the nail chewing?" She asked pulling her thumb from her mouth. A small bit of spit strung from her lip to her nail for a second.

I nodded.

"It's a nasty habit that I've had since I was little. She wiped her thumb on her sweatshirt. When you see your own mother killed by a rabid demon, you tend to develop some tics." She said like a scolded child.

"I'm sure," I said in a pathetic attempt to comfort her.

We trudged forward in the bright white heat. I observed her while she walked, she had no sleeves and wore shorts. I wondered if she wandered out here all the time, why she didn't cover herself up to protect from the sun.

Again, she caught my look. Her cherry lips parted in a sigh.

"I know what you're thinking. But, I'll take breathable clothes over suffocation. That shit you're wearing is going to get old fast. Plus, that patch is a big fat blinking beacon to the gangs." She pointed at my shoulder.

I stopped for a moment and ripped the patch off, looking at it again. The horned skull resembled a human, but much more macabre. The grin twisted upward at the corners, giving it an evil appearance. Kind of like if you let Tim Burton decide the angles. The eye that hung from its mouth dripped blood from the bottom, the type of symbol natives used to ward off any passersby. A tried and true tactic. To me though, it just looked like a sad sign of someone who had lost their way in life and turned to a bad group to fit in, or to survive. They should all consider death if they couldn't find their true peace. I spun the patch into the wind. It whipped into a vortex, and deftly disappeared into the horizon.

"That building is where I want to go." I pointed out a structure in the distance. It leaned awkwardly to the right, like a shard of glass that landed point down into the ground. The surrounding area looked like a ghetto of sorts. A makeshift wall surrounded it. Most likely made of aluminum. The wave pattern on the wall gave off odd reflections in the endless barrage of white light. I shaded my eyes with my hand.

"That place is Abysm," she pointed. "I suppose it's as good as any right now."

"I hope they have socks." I said as my feet throbbed.

She smirked and walked onwards.

The glass building gleamed in the sunlight, another irritant to me. I couldn't stand this white light, much less stomach the constant reflections. It reminded me of the asshole who invented the paisley pattern. Who approved of that moronic venture? You couldn't glance at it without getting partially blinded.

Coming upon the Abysm, the world around us fell into a hushed silence. The wind, our only companion here, vibrated off the aluminum wall. It hummed loudly as we stood there. I noticed large steel stakes erected from the ground, each one had a chain attached that rattled in the wind. The pockmarked sand showed many scorch marks. The sand itself had turned into glass bases. I momentarily pictured some poor soul who stood there, being burned to death from some unknown source above. The ashes just blown away in the wind and forgotten. My daydream halted as a loud voice boomed out from seemingly everywhere at once. "WHO. ARE. YOU?" The voice asked punctuating each word.

"Just let us in you mook!" Maddy yelled back with her hands cupped around her mouth.

I looked on intrigued as well as entertained by her comical reaction.

This must have ruffled someone's feathers because the voice became much louder and far more authoritative than before.

"IF. YOU. WANT. IN. YOU. MUST. ANSWER. THE. QUESTION!"

Maddy threw he head back and groaned loudly.

"This fucking guy," she muttered under her breath. I watched as she launched into a truly hilarious display.

"IIIIIIIII----   AMMMMMMMMMM---"   she motioned with wide gestures for dramatic effect. "MMMAAAADDDDDDDDDDDDYYYYYYYY" she said panting with effort.

Silence.

"AND. WHO. IS. HE?" The voice asked in its original volume.

She gestured to me to answer by waving her hands towards the center of the wall.

I looked at her apprehensively.

"Reese." I lied.

"YOU. ARE. NOT. REESE!" The voice boomed.

"Is this really necessary?" I placed my hands on my hips.

"YES. NONE. MAY. ENTER. WHO. ARE. THE. UNAWARE!"

Then it came to me. I knew my real name. I don't know how or why it had come to me. Fate decided to let me in on the secret. I didn't learn where I had been, what I had done, or how I came to be in this current spot, but I did suddenly know my name.

"I am Khadim Gray." I placed my hand to my chest.

The very ground shook where we stood. I kept my footing while Maddy fell onto her backside. You would think she might have been prepared for this, seeing as she was the one that had been here before. A line formed a square around us, we were on a lift of sorts. Sand poured through the opening lines down into the abyss below. A loud clank sounded as the world fell from underneath us.

The light of the world shrank as the vast square dwindled into a small window of light above us. The smell changed from dry air with a sulfur tinge, to a bevy of scents. Cooked meat, clove, sweat, and beer. Quite the transition from above.

Maddy struggled to her feet again. The platform wheeled downward, and the world blurred as the platform spun around. There were no handholds or rails to grab onto as we rotated rapidly. Maddy gave up on standing , she sat down and held on as best as she could as we descended below.

Colorful lights flashed in all directions, vertigo set in, leaving me disoriented. Suddenly a jarring thud on the bottom of the platform had me reeling forward. The spinning slowed and eventually came to a halt. I placed my hands on my knees and tried to stave off the nausea. The room snapped shut above us with a click. The platform had stopped, but my head remained foggy on determining the whereabouts of up and down.

I heard Maddy vomit, the remains from her stomach splattered across the gunmetal platform. The sand previously there, blew off in our descent only to be replaced by water and the sickly smell of bile.

"You OK?" I put my hand on her back.

She belched loudly. "I am now," she said as she wiped her mouth.

My vision slowly returned. In front of us stood a passageway, a large tunnel with loud thumping noises emanating from somewhere deep within. "We're here." She waved an unenthusiastic hand around indicating our surroundings. "Abysm, the pit of the world."

"Ah, hence the descent. I should have taken the name more literally." I considered aloud scratching my bearded chin, I pulled my goggles up onto my forehead. Without the sun beating down they were ridiculously dark.

She had begun to amble into the tunnel. I gathered myself and followed closely behind her.

The hammering pulse ahead became clearer as we went. I think they were chanting? Seemed as though they repeated a name, Pogo.

The sound grew louder. A crowd boomed loudly POGO, POGO, POGO! They did it in a quick rhythm of threes. POGO, POGO, POGO! Maddy looked at me as she backed up and gave me the lead. Unfortunately for her, I had no clue what to do either. We walked onward.

Only one way to go, forward. I took each step with purpose. After five or so minutes, and multiple turns, the temperature dropped at least ten degrees. It felt as we were going deeper into the earth.

We finally came across the entryway ahead. Flies and vermin littered the floors, many scattered upon our approach. Beyond that, bodies lay strewn across the concrete floor. Dead rotting carcasses stacked on top of one another all around the room. The floor lay saturated in blood and bile.

My eyes watered. The smell reminded me of my time locked away. I clasped my hand over my mouth to keep the taste that came with the smell at bay. Maddy made sick on the floor again. Poor girl would need to rehydrate soon, I couldn't imagine she had too many fluids left inside her...

"It...wasn't like this...before." She mentioned through back shaking retches.

I nodded and stepped over the corpses. I had trouble with my footing as I slipped on the gore. The tunnel opened wide into a vaulted room. Once Maddy and I navigated our way into the ten by ten space, we heard a grating metal on metal sound. It was a trap, we walked for ages to get into a damned trap. Shit.

The wall behind us slammed as the door above dropped into place. One of the corpses wasn't totally out of the way, and splashed gore all over the room as the door turned it into pulp. Maddy shrieked and wriggled like she stepped through a spider web, as body parts splashed onto her exposed legs. It missed me for the most part, but my boots were already covered in the remains anyways.

I looked up and saw the single brass window with a dimpled piece of acrylic in front of it. It reminded me of the mask of one of those diving suits you always saw in movies. Like Jacques Cousteau would wear on his deep-sea expeditions. I assumed they could see through it, but we were unable to see them.

No idea though, truly odd, not that the place stood as the picture of normality. Maddy pointed to a speaker on the wall, a circular metal disc with small black lines in it. This is where the source of the chanting resided. The loop played over and over.

Moving closer, it sounded tinny without any source of bass. The repetitive cadence triggered a migraine. It's possible the tunnel had speakers in it also, to amplify the sound.

The small window opened and the speaker shut off. Instant relief for my throbbing head. A silhouette of a thin man with wiry hair sat behind the window. Simply seeing another human relieved my stress, even if he may be some lunatic that trapped us in here. Truly impossible to tell anything else about him through this window.

"KHADIM. MADDY." He clicked his moist tongue.

"WHAT. DO. YOU. OFFER. FOR. PASSAGE."

"Ugh…" Maddy shrugged at me.

As she grunted, a metal drawer sprung from the wall in a loud whoosh. It clicked and rang out as it popped up.

Maddy jumped back and eyeballed it suspiciously.

I looked back at the still warm pile of bodies oozing on the floor and considered that I should go with something good here.

I reached into my jacket pocket and placed the empty flare gun in the drawer. Maddy gawked at me with her wide emerald eyes, her eyebrows tilted in disapproval.

"Really? The fucking gun? Of all things to put in a damned drawer…" she trailed off as she rummaged through her purse.

She then placed a Rhapsody soda into the metal drawer.

The door snapped shut with a click.

We heard a slight giggle behind the window.

"PLEASED. RHAPSODY. FIZZY. ENTER."

The wall itself separated and clicked open, the air warmed became more breathable immediately. Light flooded the room, and we saw some semblance of the innards of the underground Abysm. The walls yawned open fully to greet us with a passage into the core of the city.

Inhaling deeply, I closed my eyes to take in the full essence of this place. My mouth salivated at the welcoming scent of fresh food. The smell of other people was a sensation I enjoyed revisiting. Each scent redolent of a time past. I opened my eyes and took a step forward next to Maddy.

"Well, that was a pain in the ass." She groaned. "I'm fucking hungry."After being locked away in a basement with the loving smell of feces, urine, and the coppery tang of blood to tease your senses, this was truly paradise. Hundreds of discussions echoed throughout, and I could hear people moving all around the walkways. The doorway snapped shut behind us. We moved forward through a hallway that gave way to a sprawling market.

The caverns of Abysm were immense. Terracotta colored stone vaulted upwards and out of sight, like having a beautiful view of a city at night. Sparkling lights flickered on and off at random for what could be miles. Hundreds of people shopped at a multitude of stores in the bustling marketplace.

From the top of the hill where the hallway had ended, I saw a man selling grilled animal carcasses. Next door to him there stood a shack that had its rusted awning pulled open. Makeshift weapons laid out across the counter, in front of a large bar filled to the brim with a melting pot of people, and in all this madness, there it stood, in all its glory. A clothing store. They had to have socks.

"I'm going to the..." I went to tell Maddy, but realized she had already headed over to the man peddling meats. I decided to venture over to the clothing store on my own.

I walked past some large men, who had some modifications done to their faces. I couldn't help but stare, I had never seen the likes of this. One had a prominent metal jaw, the other donned an arm made from wrought iron. All of them were covered in dirt and sweat. I could almost see the odor pouring off of them. I watched the man with the iron arm lift and crush a beer can with his hand. His group laughed together. The whole piercings movement had really been taken to a new level. I wonder if Hot Topic sells those things.

"It's all fully functional, mmhmm," said a sweet voice, coming from a petite middle-aged lady wearing jade tea glasses beside me. She stood in an ocher coverall with the sleeves rolled up. "Been making em' for years. I'm Patty. I'm sweet, talented, and expensive as hell." She chuckled. I saw as she tilted her head back in the laugh, that she had a tattoo that said Patty on her neck.

Her laugh brought back memories for me. Something I felt I'd lost. I pictured an older lady sitting in a rocking chair with an open door behind her. She slowly rocked back and forth while she sang an old Cat Stevens song. She had weathered dark piercing brown eyes, but the warmest smile you could imagine. My eyes welled as I reminisced about her.

I must have been visibly lost because Patty grabbed my arm. "Dear, are you ok?" She smiled. "You made it in, you mustn't worry any longer about that damned Pogo. He does all that nonsense for show anyhow. All that POGO, POGO, POGO…" she waved a hand, and dismissed it. "You're new." She nodded and squinted through her glasses at me.

"I need socks." I explained to her at a loss of what else to say. "My feet are going to crawl out of my boots and stab me in the throat soon if I don't." I sat down and removed a boot and saw that my feet were red and swollen from their travels. They could have been worse I guess, but they were still in pain.

"Mmhmm…Patchwork is over there. It's the cheapest clothing store we have." She pointed to the shop I had originally headed to before I ran into her. She chuckled again. "Well, if your feet fall off, I can replace em' right quick!" She held up a handsaw, that she produced from seemingly nowhere.

I opened my eyes wide in shock and shook my head.

"Thanks." I said to her. "I'll be on my way. Enjoy your peace." I nodded to her and turned through the crowded streets, walking barefoot and carrying my boots in hand. So much more comfortable.

I thought about Patty for a second, she had a golden aura. I'd never seen a golden aura before. Typically, auras ranged in more muted colors. Metallic colors were something I was wholly unfamiliar with, I didn't get a bad feeling from her though, so she must have been alright. My instincts were rarely wrong.

I walked up to the store with the pulsing sign that said PATCHWORK, in glimmering silver letters. A man wearing a backwards sweatshirt stood outside. It covered the bottom half of his face, but I noticed it went around his head entirely. The top of his head sat exposed.

He wore slotted sunglasses that were large on his face and he had a mohawk shaved close to his skull.

His arms jangled as he spoke to customers and waved his arms. Tinny bands that clinked and tinkled as he shifted. Minor blemishes of thievery and lying littered his aura. Something I would expect from a true businessman.

He sauntered up to me, stood straight up and put a hand across his chest and another to his chin. "Hmmmmmmm…" he lulled, hanging onto the m for what seemed ages. "I'm going to jump out of the ordinary here and say that you need socks…" He opened his arms to illustrate his point.

"An astute observation," I mentioned.

He scoffed as he tilted his chin downwards in a nod. "We have many socks. I even have a six pack around here somewhere." He waved a hand as he leaned over to my ear and whispered. "Still in the package. Freshhhhhh." He opened his flattened palms and pulled them out laterally. I liked socks, but didn't regard them in such a high form of fashion as this guy might have.

"I'll take a single pair," I said as his face fell into annoyance. He seemed disappointed I didn't want all of them. If he knew that my current hobby was stealing clothes from people I killed, he might have been thrilled to part with a simple pair of socks.

He sauntered to a section of his kiosk and pointed out the sock basket. "They're available for fifty partials or trade." He noted.

"Partials?" I asked him quizzically.

He cocked an eyebrow over his glasses. "Money. Honey." He did the things with his hands again. The jingling rung out.

"As in cash? I have…" I pulled out the wallet I had taken from Anthony in the shop. There were the three pathetic, sweaty, and crinkled up dollar bills. They looked like you could catch a virus just from handling them.

"Oh my." He flailed his hands. "Put that away." He smarted and patted my hands down. "Do you think I have change for something like that here?"

I stood dumbfounded, and utterly lost.

"Just take it."

I pushed the balled-up cash into his hands.

"You really don't mind?" He twisted his head inspecting me with one extremely suspicious eye. "That's a lot of money."

"If it's that much, give me the pack of socks."

"Done!" He chortled gaily and stuffed the cash into a pocket somewhere in his shirt.

I stood silently while he handed me a bag of socks, a black trucker cap, to which I politely declined, a carton of cigarettes, a pistol with a full clip, and a box of bullets. He placed it all neatly into a reusable bag that said Juicy on the side of it. He looked up at me and took his sunglasses off. He had tears in his eyes.

"You have made me so happy today." He said as he grabbed a metal pole with a hook on the end. I guessed he was closing the shop down for the day. He hooked the handle above us and turned to me before shutting it.

"If you EVER need anything, you come see me," he spoke over his shoulder, his voice filled with compassion.

"Patchy will get you whatever you need."

"Thanks." I said with a raised eyebrow. I'm not sure how I got all this stuff, but he seemed to care greatly about the three dollars. Good for him. I was glad I could make somebody's day in this sideshow.

I felt a tap on my shoulder. I turned to see Maddy standing there with a large leg of meat in each hand. She extended one to me. It smelled gamey, like it had turned a day or so ago.

"Here, got you food. It's cheap enough down here. Cost me a penny for both," she said.

"I even got change." She held up a handful of iron coins. Upon inspection, they were about half the size of a dime, with a hole in the center.

"They're called partials." She smiled. "They break a penny into a hundred. The penny is the new dollar. Figured you may not know that because you've been sleeping or whatever." she shrugged as she tore a big bite into her meat.

I turned and saw that my new friend Patchy had disappeared into a now closed storefront.

That figured. I woke up and had a fortune, and I blew it on a pack of socks. I decided to keep my mishap to myself, as not to make Maddy vomit, roll her eyes, or chew her nails. Best to let her eat and be happy, sans tics.

She handed me some partials and told me to grab us some beers. She sat at an open table and I dropped my bag of goods down next to her. There were lots of people there that had normal auras, but a few had truly grotesque auras. Something I would like to handle, but in that place, it wasn't the safest venture to partake in for sure. This world had too many struggling people who were fighting for happiness and shouldn't be placed in a dangerous situation to make improper decisions that might involve them.

The bartender stood tall with her purple hair in a ponytail. Her amber eyes gleamed when the light hit them. Her shapely lips matched the color of her hair. She grinned and asked what I wanted.

"A beer and a water." I leaned onto the bar.

She smirked and raised an eyebrow. "High roller huh?" She gave me a wink and pulled out two clean glasses. They were pint glasses with the Abysm symbol etched into them. She placed them under the gear capped taps and pulled.

A golden amber flowed from the beer tap, while the water tap featured an ice cube for its symbol. I watched her fill my glass with water. I had never seen a more beautiful thing after my trek. I noticed that there were no ice cubes placed in the glass.

"Ice?" I tilted my head and grinned hopefully.

"It's cold," she said to me with a matter of fact look. "Don't have room to make ice and waste water like that. Abysm rules. Sorry." She gave me an apologetic look.

I looked around the bar and noticed a man hunched over the bar. Hulking and morbid looking, a living tumor that had latched onto the bar itself. Far larger than a normal man, probably close to seven-foot-tall and wider than a Buick. His flesh was misshapen probably from burns, and he modeled a few iron brads pierced into his face, possibly for intimidation. I doubted it existed to hold his face together. Which struck me as funny, because his intimidation never once came into question for me. I couldn't take my eyes off of him. This man stood out from the others, as a lion stood out amongst kittens. His aura circulated jet-black and saturated with sins. He wore an armored jacket complete with large iron shoulder domes and iron plates around his ribs. "Hon?" the bartender snapped me out of my stare. "I wouldn't be doing that to him." She glanced with her eyes at the man I observed. "He might have your eyes, or your whole head for looking at him wrong."

She smiled widely and said, "Seventy partials please." I looked over at Maddy who was already elbow deep in her food. I paid the girl what I had. "Thank you very much! Enjoy your water and beer!" She smiled and moved onto the next customer.

I had not noticed the large man eyeballing me as I moved to the table.

"Here." I placed her beer down on the table and started to drink my water.

"Thanks." she said as she stuck out a greasy hand, grabbed her beer, and began to drink mid chew.

After a few seconds, she downed her beer, and looked at me, her eyebrows furrowed into a scowl.

I had done something wrong.

"Really? You can't ask before you blow my cash on water?" she pointed at the frosted glass accusingly.

"Didn't know it was expensive." I said as I leaned back shrugging.

"Most water is so horribly toxic from the Devil's moves back in the days that it's rare to find a clean spring anymore. Luckily, Abysm happens to have the world's largest one. What'd you pay for it? Fifty partials?"

I nodded in affirmation.

"Sounds about right, but that's one hell of a price for water still."

I shrugged again. Without any warning, Maddy leaned over and placed her elbows on the table and launched into a story. Not even a primer, bam. Storytime. She loved doing this.

"You see, the Devil and God hated each other, and the Devil hated humans almost as much as he hated God." She said taking a bite off her meat and continuing her story, undaunted by the chunks of flesh in her mouth.

"He decided to kill us, he would release more of his infamous plagues. I mean, not that they were HIS original idea, he stole them from God, but whatever." She paused in thought.

"Ok, so anyways. There was this war, right? God and the Devil duked it out, with earth as their arena." She swallowed.

"One, this is cool because we learned that God indeed existed, yet unfortunate because this meant the Devil did too." She motioned for a waitress to come over in between her story.

"Beer me!" She tossed the waitress some partials on her tray The waitress hustled off to the bar.

I drank my water while I listened to her.

"Ok, so there were Angels who fought for God, and Demons who fought for the Devil. Simple, but those two aren't known for playing fair, right? So, the Devil began to kill off humans by poisoning our water supply, this would turn those dead people into hosts for demons.

"They would fall as parents, children, etc. Then they would arise as demons, misshapen things with fangs and claws and such." She made pointy motions with her fingers in front of her mouth to simulate what teeth might look like, provided they were made of fingers.

"Some of them had wings, a great disadvantage to the angels. Seeing as humans are God's children, he didn't want this to happen to them so he decided to turn the sun white." She paused for effect.

"Why would that matter? Pfff- fuck if we humans knew, but demons would explode in pure white light. Like fucking..." She motioned widely with her hands and made booming noise. Spittle flew from her mouth onto the table.

"Something biblical or such. Each passing day the demons would die out. This angered the Devil, so he decided to stop the earth's very rotation."

As I tried keeping up with her endless barrage, the waitress returned with a beer for Maddy. She smiled at her and drank that one down just as fast as the previous one. I started to think that the use of oxygen might just be optional for her.

"Ok. So, here's the snag with stopping the earth's rotation. First thing that happened? Lots of humans died instantly, because when it stopped, it caused us to realize we were coasting with wicked momentum. You know how you ride in a car, but don't realize it because you're sitting in the car? Well, if you were driving a huge earth-mobile…" she used her glass as a demonstration, "and you crashed into a mountain at say," she paused and tapped her chin. "nine hundred plus miles per hour." She smashed the glass into the table, it shattered all over. I glanced around, but no one seemed to care. "It'd fucking hurt, right? Probably just destroy the car, the people inside of it, and everyone else in the surrounding area."

She plopped back into her seat and leaned forward again.

"So yeah, shit tons of people died in that instant. The people who were least affected by that phase lived at the North and South Pole. So, Santa lived on just fine and fucking dandy, while the rest of us assholes who live in the normal part of the world were smashed into dust. Not everyone died, but a shit ton did. Luckily all I got was some scrapes and bruises from it, I've always been resilient. Our car didn't make it though, and my Dad broke his arm."

"Obviously, anyone in friendly skies flying or whatever didn't even notice." She stopped to wipe her mouth and put down her half-eaten food. She looked over and noticed I hadn't touched mine.

"Are you not hungry?" She asked with concern in her voice.

"I'm giving you my full attention, and I don't like to chew and listen. They conflict with one another." I explained to her.

She had a wide grin on her face. I could see some pepper stuck between her teeth.

"So you do have some 'tics' too then!" she smirked and made the quotation symbols with her hands.

I shook my head with a smirk.

I corrected her on this.

"A tic is a motor function, something involuntary, like rolling your eyes, clearing your throat, biting your nails, etc. What I have is called courtesy, an act of consideration. At worst, it's a pet peeve to listen and chew for me. So, you are incorrect."

She rolled her eyes and tilted her head back dramatically.

"So anyways, look, back to my story." She continued unperturbed by my counter banter.

"The earth isn't, well wasn't totally round, right? So, when the Devil stopped its rotation, the earth rounded out, since we were spinning all the time, the earth itself used to bulge at the equator. Now, it doesn't. Not a problem, right?" She smiled with a glint of mischief in her eyes. Then her face turned into a mask of anger.

She slammed her hand on the table. "Wrong! This caused the oceans to unsettle! They poured outward onto the north and south poles, so guess what?!" She threw her hands into the air with her eyes wide.

"Santa fucking drowned! It's bullshit! Just pisses me off thinking about it. I guess that we're ok here in the middle now, but the other problem is that since we don't spin any longer, we no longer have seasons, so Santa wouldn't have a job anyhow." As she sat back in her seat, she summoned the waitress again, the girl already had a beer in her hand. Maddy paid her. She slammed down that beer as well, some dribbled down her chin into the fabric of her shirt.

Maddy looked dazed for a moment. The alcohol finally seemed to be hitting her.

"Sooo, as you can see. We're fucked man! Only people who get some sort of normality, are those rich assholes in Ouroboros. That *magical* city." she waved her hands dramatically.

I took a sip of water and stopped mid-swallow. Maddy gaped at something or someone behind me, her entire face draining of color. She squeaked out the words. "Oh shit."

I turned to see the living tumor in green standing behind me. He breathed heavily in my face, looked down at me and said in a voice made of grinding stones. "Nice jacket."

I looked up at him, unperturbed by his size. "Thank you, it's new." I said patting the lapels.

His solid black eyes reminded me of something Nietzsche said, "When you gaze into the abyss, it gazes into you." We made eye contact for a moment. Much to my surprise, he visibly shuddered.

He shoved past the crowds, knocking others to the floor as he went.

Maddy spit as she shouted at me, "That's fucking Faul man!" She frantically grabbed her things from the table, including my leg of meat. Even terror couldn't deter her endless hunger.

I turned to her. "He's the leader of that biker gang?" I pointed at him as he walked off.

"He's a fucking living God man!" she said.

I noticed she cursed a lot when plastered, possibly when sober too.

"We have got to go; I'm amazed he didn't kill you right then and there!" she snapped.

I sat back down, dusted my feet off, and pulled on some fresh socks. They even had that wonderful elastic feel, when they fit your feet just right. I must have been smiling because Maddy commented.

"You look like an idiot. Get your fucking socks on and let's bolt. I don't want him coming back here, realizing you killed one of his guys, stole his clothes. He'll try to kill us." She said probably louder than she should have, the beer acted as an amplifier for her vocal chords.

Aside from a few shifting chairs, the bar fell silent. I already knew the scenario at hand. I strapped my boots, stood up, and without looking at who came from behind me, I grabbed my iron stool and spun full force into the oncoming adversary.

He didn't expect it and his jawbone exploded under the impact. The dude's head snapped backwards. He landed flat on his back. I placed my weight on my back foot and dropped my heel into his oversized throat. Oh, how I loved that satisfying crack under my boot. No one would miss him.

I turned to see his fellow goons charging at me. I swung my stool at the one with the crooked schnoz. He reached up and pried it from my hands with his iron arm. The metal grated loudly as the stool became scrap in his hands. Steam hissed from his arm. I used my free hand to pull out the pistol in my bag.

He wrenched the stool from my grip. I let go and shot him three times in the chest.

I could see a terrified red-headed bartender through the holes in his chest. She screamed out. The dude fell backwards and collapsed onto the ground. Another favor done for the world.

I found my footing when I spotted the other two guys stomping toward me with bats in their gigantic hands. I leveled the pistol and shot the larger in his knee. He toppled over and squealed in pain.

The blond closed in and cracked me with his aluminum bat across my left shoulder.

Bam! He smacked me in my ribs and neck. I hunched over to fight the pain. He loomed over me, I shot straight up as fast as I could and slammed my head into his jaw.

He teetered backwards. My head ached horribly. It felt like I stood straight up into a steel girder. Warm blood spilled down my cheeks. His metal jaw had split my skull open, clearly not my finest maneuver of the day.

Blood trickled onto my lips. I wiped my face with my forearm and leveled the pistol at him. I felt like I looked like a madman right now.

The gun kicked as I fired it. The bullet blazed into his right arm, it fell limply to his side. He grabbed his shoulder and whimpered, his aura showed he didn't deserve to die.

I left him and walked over to the larger man I'd shot in the knee, his aura told a vastly different story. I stood over him, blood continuing to stream down my face, and I watched as he writhed in pain.

His aura had a russet brown tinge with a cerulean spot. He had killed a child, one of the worst things humans are capable of. Children are innocent, with many years before they comprehend the real decisions that impact themselves and others. The vision seeped into my mind.

He stood there yelling at a small boy with messy brown hair. He could not have been more than six years old. A broken window gaped behind the boy and as he picked up the pieces of glass, runnels of deep crimson blood trailed down his hands and arms to the ground. The carpet sanguine from the blood. The boy tried to stifle his sobs. In the man's hand smoldered a fireplace poker. He smiled at the boy and raised the weapon above his head.

The strong sharp, pungent taste of gun powder brought my senses back to the present.

Tears in my eyes, I ground my teeth, fighting for control of my emotions. My jaw ached as I turned my attention to him.

"That child you killed will never get a chance to grow up. It's unfair that you get to live and continue your horrible ways, while he never got a chance to make his own decisions, you decided his fate over a broken window? A WINDOW?!"

The gun bucked as I shot him in the other knee. "He couldn't have been older than six." A loud report rang out as I shot him in the stomach. He coughed up blood and tears ran down his face.

"Worst of all, he was your own son." The gun issued forth one last tremor as I shot him in the throat. He lied there in a growing pool of blood, while everyone stared at me. I wiped the tears as they rolled down my face.

Maddy stood horrified, but calm. She had tears in her eyes as well. She placed a hand on my shoulder. "Come on Khadim. We have to go."

We turned, and fled into the streets of Abysm.

CHAPTER 4

AN ALLY EMERGES

WE RAN THROUGH Abysm.

My head ached. Blood and sweat distorted my vision, and my adrenaline was the only thing that kept my legs churning. The once exciting smells of food, cloves, and alcohol were replaced with the smell of our own acrid sweat and dust that kicked up as we ran.

We sprinted through hordes of people. Everywhere we ran people watched. They offered no help. They stood back and judged us from a distance. No one knew us, why should they place their trust in us? Why should they protect us? Every shop closed their doors to us.

We turned down an alleyway. There! A door stood agape and we charged towards it. It slammed in our face, moments before we were inside. Maddy screamed and hurled the leg of meat at the glass door. It splattered against the surface leaving a mess.

"Fuck." She noted as she kicked the ground.

We sought shelter from the impending problems that headed our way. Yet none were available.

We charged down another alleyway when we heard someone shout out "Hey, come in, come in!" We looked over and saw Patty standing there, the friendly woman from the market I met earlier. She leaned outside of a garage with a beckoning hand. "Hurry,

hurry!" Maddy turned to me with a questioning glance, and I nodded to let her know it was safe. We headed over to the open door. Patty stepped back and we crashed inside. Maddy fell over and lied on the floor panting, her chest heaved up and down.

I looked around and observed our sanctuary. A dirty garage with an old muscle car parked in one half, and the other half reserved for Maddy's hurried breath.

"Thanks for the shelter Patty." I said after catching my breath. "Patty, Maddy, Maddy, Patty." I motioned from one woman to the other and made introductions. I placed my hands on my knees and stood up.

Patty nodded at me and then smiled at Maddy.

"You shouldn't have killed anyone here. That was a mistake for sure." She jabbed her finger at us, like a Mother scolding her child. "Glass is going to come find you."

Great, another problem.

"Who is Glass?" I asked plainly. This is what I needed, some new asshole to add to the plethora of problems I had already afforded myself in the past hour.

"What is Glass, would be a better question," she answered. "Glass," she paused. "Is a cyborg. You know, biomechanical basically? He looks like a human, but he's mostly metal." I immediately pictured that robot cop from the movies.

"Don't you make parts for things like that?" I asked her.

She nodded at me. The conversation halted there when Maddy caught her breath.

"Fuck." Maddy heaved loudly, throwing her arms out, they slapped the ground loudly. "What the hell was that about Khadim?" She said through heavy breathing, rubbing her hands over her sweat soaked head.

"They attacked us. I killed the ones that didn't deserve to live, the other ones got to survive. They were just punks acting on someone else's authority. No doubt, that Faul character. They were Shavs correct?" I asked her.

She screwed up her face in annoyance. "Yes, they were Shavs, but killing Shavs should not be your hobby." Her long finger pointed at me. "It's dangerous shit man!"

Patty agreed with her."Shavs are horrible people and only deserve the worst." Patty said, shaking a finger at Maddy. "I'm only saying that it's dangerous to do so!"

"They inflict only pain, and use greed as motivation. That Faul is no better! Mmmhmm..." she nodded. "He's been coming around here trying to get me to install parts on his 'boys,'" she shook her head, "So they can withstand more punishment, and do more damage. Says he'll pay me enough to make me rich!" She spat a surprisingly large wad phlegm on the floor. "He can take his money and shove it up his *behind* for all I care! Patty don't work for no false God!" She said while crossing her arms.

She turned and began surveying her home.

"Now, you are clearly going to need a way out of here before Glass gets here." She stroked her long ponytail that hung over her shoulder. She looked over at the car and sighed heavily, obviously reluctant about something. I followed her eyes to the beast that sat in the garage.

"I suppose I could loan her to you." She remarked to herself as she raised an eyebrow. "I'd want her back in time though, so no roughing her up!" She said after turning to look at me, her eyes stern and terrifying.

Once again, Maddy broke the mood.

"A car? I could only dream." Maddy had somehow recovered quickly after the thought of having an automobile to ride in. "We could go to the city now Khadim." I didn't know what she was talking about, as per usual.

"A car is all well and good, but how would I get out of here? If

I had to guess, we are far below the surface." I noted while thinking about the surroundings we ran through.

"Nope." Pat remarked and dismissed my ignorance with a wave of her hand. "This here is a cave. The entrance you took to get in was just on the top side of the mountain, where we are now just so happens to have a road out of here, built by yours truly." She placed her hands on her ocher coverall collar proudly.

"Get the fuck out!" Maddy said.

The front door thundered and quaked.

Patty crept to the door and peered through the peep hole. She turned to look back at us. She had fear in her eyes.

The door exploded open. Patty's head slammed violently into the wall and she slumped over in an unconscious heap. Luckily she wasn't dead, the old woman seemed tough as nails.

"Oh ho, ho, ho…" Faul said in his grinding voice. "Come to roost in the old hen's house, have you?"

I watched as Faul stooped through the shattered door and into the garage. Fractured wooden pieces fell from the dismantled door as his boots crunched over them. A sound of slow dragging metal on concrete echoed around the room. He clutched a massive metal hammer that reminded me of a super-sized meat tenderizer. His back cracked audibly multiple times and he arched his back and stretched to his full height once inside.

Faul towered high above us. He had come alone, one of our only advantages so far. His figure took up a lot of space, an added bonus in a small shop. He'd have a hard time swinging that maul around.

"So you finally woke up, already killing my boys off too. Heh." He said pointing one knobby finger at my jacket.

What did he mean that I had woken up? Did he know who I was?

"The Constant is making big boy decisions that are upsetting the balance already. My balance." Faul roared through Patty's entryway and back into her living room.

"Things were fine until you started killing off my boys." In a split second, he had closed the distance between us.

He swung his maul overhead with ease. The concrete shattered into dust in front of me as the maul bludgeoned a crater into the floor. I jumped back while Maddy scrambled off behind Faul into the rest of the house. I had no idea where she went. The giant paid her no mind and instead hoisted his weapon up again.

"Why are you calling me a Constant? What the hell is that?" I hurriedly asked him while rolling to avoid a wide swing from the maul. I felt the air rush over my back as maul connected with the wall. He created a new bay window that overlooked the next room, an addition I'm sure Patty didn't want.

"Don't play with me boy." He said with vehemence, his breath like curdled milk. "I know you came for me, this is my territory, the Outlands are mine. Keep the big dogs out of it." The veins in his huge neck swelled as he swung again, this time tearing out the left side of the door frame.

I didn't think this place would take much more of Faul's living wrecking ball. It was time to move the fight elsewhere.

"You know that Shav you left alive?" He asked me while he turned and pulled his weapon back into his grip. "I killed him. What could I do with a wounded soldier? His usefulness had run out." He laughed a guttural laugh. "You practically did me a favor by letting him live. I felt great after I smashed his skull in!" He cracked his neck and grinned, his teeth protruding at all angles.

His aura a living pool of ichor showed he was telling the truth.

I rolled around to the front of the garage back towards the entrance, and ran further inside to gain some distance. I heard him talking to me, but I didn't turn to see if he followed, his thundering footfalls let me know.

He stomped into the living room. The house smelled like a can of WD-40. Tables covered in metal knick-knacks, gears and tools strewn about the floor in no order. It occurred to me Patty was a bit of a grease-monkey.

"I have run this territory for years, I'm not going to let you mess with that." He snapped at me, curling his ham-sized fist in front of him.

"Look, I don't give a shit what you're doing here. I just wanted to get some socks and leave." I told him honestly.

"Do not lie to me." His wretched breath overpowered the oily odor in the air.

He stuck his chin out perfectly for me. Finally, an opening, I leaned in and placed my fist right in the sweet spot. It felt like hitting a vault door.

My fist rocked and my bones rattled down to my feet. I must have looked like one of those old Tex Avery cartoons. My whole body vibrated back and forth.

He staggered back a step or two, enough for me to tackle him back into the garage, where he tripped on the debris from the door. He landed on his back and slid supine. I realized Maddy had returned and stood right over him. Her left hand held a golden spray can, and in her right hand, a black one.

"Hey Faul, time for a makeover asshole!" she chanted at him.

He opened his eyes in surprise and looked up at Maddy. This time he made the wrong move.

She aimed both cans towards his face and pressed the nozzles. The cans erupted right into Faul's face. Streams of black and gold mist intertwined. The paint ran down his face in thick lines. "AAAAAGGGHHHHHH…" he screamed out. His hammer clanged loudly as it dropped, and he grabbed for his face.

Gold and black runnels ran down his face, and all over his hands. He looked like a glam kid from the seventies. *Well played Maddy.*

"Let's go! I've got the keys!" Maddy shouted.

I ran back to the entryway and deftly scooped up Patty. I

carried her over to the car. The top was down, and I placed her in the backseat. Maddy climbed into the driver's seat. She looked down and slapped the dashboard in dismay.

"What?" I asked her as I wondered what the holdup could be.

"Stick? I can't fucking drive stick. My first car in years and it's a fucking stick. God damn it." She stomped her feet.

"Move, I can drive." I said. "I used to have a Volkswagen Bug back in the days."

"How old are you man?" Maddy asked while she reluctantly slid onto the passenger seat.

"I have no idea. These memories are all over the place." I told her honestly.

Faul howled and rolled up to his feet rubbing his face violently. He looked over at the sound and I could see one of his black orbs stare at us with hatred. Having gained at least a little bit of vision, he charged the car like a bull, head down and at full speed.

The car roared to life and I took his moment's hesitation to barrel backwards through the garage door. People dove out of the way as we blasted through the gate. The garage door rolled off the side of the car and onto the dirt.

I had no idea where I could drive to, and why the hell so many people were around. I didn't have time to think. I saw Faul charging wildly into the street after us. His gold and black face twisted into a rage, you could almost taste his fury.

I made my decision as I tore off down the street ahead, clueless as to if I have made the right choice in direction or not. The opposite direction from Faul had to be the right way in my opinion.

We left Faul in the dust as he stood covered in spray paint screaming obscenities at us. I peeked into the rearview mirror and watched him slam his maul into the ground. Dirt kicked up into his face as he screamed out for revenge.

Maddy pouted in the passenger seat. Her arms crossed over her chest.

"Are you serious? We just escaped death and you're pissed because you can't drive?"

"Yes. It's a fucking 69' Roadrunner man. I've only seen sim-screens of this car, much less had a chance to drive one." She exhaled loudly, like a petulant child.

"68' Dear." we heard Patty say from the backseat. "You already dented up the rear end by the way." She groaned.

"I do appreciate the lifesaving and all though," Patty said as she sat up. She looked over at Maddy and hit her on the shoulder. "Buckle up you ninny, are you trying to fly out of the car and become roadkill?"

Maddy looked at her wide-eyed and buckled her seatbelt. "How about those moves back there? I blinded Faul with the spray paint. Pretty clever huh? I found them in your office. If that's what you want to call it, it was a mess in there."

"I've got no lady to impress anymore. What does cleanliness matter?" Her eyes watered and lost their focus. She turned her head towards the window, she seemed forlorn.

"Turn right up here," she said, pointing ahead at an opening.

I turned where she had indicated. The road nothing but gravel, truly horrible stuff to drive on, it kicked up an awful mess as we went. The tunnels were dark, but aside from the onslaught of gravel, not too bad. No one was trying to kill us, and no one accused me of being a Constant. Whatever the hell that was.

Not that that meant anything to me at all. Only a sliver of this world had made much sense so far. Last I could remember; David Bowie had just come out. Why did I know that name?

Things were crazy. Being tied to a gurney and having your organs removed at least had some sort of an order to it.

"Stop here." Patty said to me.

I slowed the car to a stop, the engine idled quietly.

She got up and opened the car door, I noted the doors opened the opposite way of normal car doors. Suicide doors.

Upon reaching the rock wall, she felt along the stones. She then twisted her knuckles and her pointer finger produced a light. I smirked. I'll be damned if this old woman wasn't full of surprises. She moved it around the wall for a moment and found her objective.

"There." She said enthusiastically, and tapped the wall and a panel opened. She twisted some things and pushed an object out of my vision, and I went blind again as the light poured in. I would never get used to that sun.

An immense gateway lifted upwards into the mountain, well hidden in plain sight. The sun shone so bright white my eyes watered again. I hated this sun. We drove out and Patty walked through and shut the door from a panel on the front of the wall. A crafty thing, no telling what else this woman had contributed to the world.

Patty limped over to the driver side, I could tell her injuries bothered her.

"What's she doing?" Maddy asked fiddling with her nails.

"I don't think she's going with us," I told her.

Patty walked up to me and placed her warm hand on my arm. It was a rough hand, calloused over many times. "You have been recognized as a Constant, the pursuit will be strong for you. You need to remember to keep your own peace above all else and succeed where so many have failed," she said. "Don't be swayed by others."

"What do you mean?" I asked her.

"Just be you, that's all," she said, without skipping a beat she continued. This was one of those tactics Mothers and Fathers would use when they knew they had said too much, but didn't want you to ask any more questions. "There are some things about Pearl you should know."

"Pearl another Cyborg?!" Maddy asked looking around for possible bad guys in the distance.

She gestured to the car and rubbed her hand lovingly on the side. "No, she's the car," she said sternly to Maddy who had clearly interrupted.

"So, Pearl here is solar powered. You won't need gas in her, ever. Unless of course you go to the Dark, then you'll need gas, but she has a reserve tank that's full just in case. She's armor plated, and the top does come back on. She also has a nice radio that plays whatever songs you can remember. Just wave your hand in front of the stereo to turn it on. It'll connect to whoever waves. It's a neurological connection, you might feel spacey at first, but it'll pass," she mentioned. "There are some knick-knacks in the trunk for you too."

"Other than that just be safe. I'll expect my car back at some point. You should take care of yourself now. Get away from Faul and the others. They'll try to change you, or flat out kill you. There is much more to you than you know." she said while smiling. "I'm glad you finally got out. Go find Solace, she's in Ouroboros. She'll be able to explain to you what a Constant is. Good woman that Solace is, always looking out for others."

I looked at her. I didn't know who she was really, or why she continued being so kind, but it was enough to move me.

"I'll be back with your car. I must find myself." I hated to leave her behind.

Maddy already waved her hand enthusiastically in front of the stereo. Some loud metal music came on. It jarred me out of my thoughts.

"This is awesome!" Maddy shouted over the music.

I turned back to say goodbye and thank Patty, but she had already vanished. Not sure how an old woman could move that fast, but I'd seen stranger things I suppose.

"What the hell is an Ouroboros?" I asked Maddy.

CHAPTER 5
THE NEW TOYS

WE DROVE FOR hours in the blistering sun. After a hundred miles or so we pulled over to the side of the dusty road and figured out how to put the top back on. Old cinema would have had you believe roasting in the sun with the top down could be loads of fun. I would equate it more along the lines of sticking your head inside a piping hot oven.

The heat fluctuated between one hundred and fifteen to a hundred and twenty degrees. The wind remained elusive and there could be no telling where the next water source might be. I couldn't recall the last time I saw a lake, river, or even a bottle of water for that matter. So, the top had to be on or I could've possibly died of heat exhaustion.

When we were figuring out the roof, I decided to stop and take a look at the car. It had sable white and powder blue interior. The tires were all terrain, fat, knobby, and tough. I imagined them to have some sort of defense mechanism for flats in this environment.

I walked to the back, and popped open the trunk. Saying I was surprised would be an understatement. I found way more than just a few knick-knacks, as Patty said. Weapons, rations, and water bottles. Of course, hydration in the trunk the entire time. Life continued to be consistently ironic like that.

I leaned down and pulled the water from its confines in a cold fridge built into the base of the trunk. I counted six bottles as I twisted the top off. They were plastic containers, like the ones I used to drink from, before I dabbled as a human experiment.

The cool water slid down my throat and my insides went frosty for a far too fleeting moment. Being fairly certain I didn't need to have water, I still greatly enjoyed imbibing the liquid joy. In fact, it was the purest I had tasted since awakening.

Possibly filtered back in Patty's home. The woman had achieved sainthood in my mind from this. Maddy came over to me complaining. Of course, always complaining.

"Are you almost done..." she trailed off when she saw the open trunk. She snagged the bottle from my hand and took a swig before pouring the rest over her head. It ran down the back of her neck and down her sweatshirt. She shook violently. "Wow that's cold," she shrieked with glee. "Still, I needed that. Haven't had a bath in weeks," she said as she chortled, shaking the excess water from her hair.As she looked over in the trunk, her eyes went wide. She wiped her wet cheeks with her arm.

"Holy shitsnacks! That's the best-looking thing I've seen in years!" She reached over and grabbed a black machete with a long silver edge. It came with a black holster. She undid her belt and slapped it on across her left thigh, cinching it tight.

"You're left handed." I mentioned after taking note of which leg she put it on.

She looked up at me, her thick eyebrow raised in a curl.

"I write with my right hand, and fight with my left. Does that make me a southpaw?" She said squinting through her goggles in contemplation.

"It makes you ambidextrous." I said.

"I suppose it does." She smiled widely. "You?"

"Left handed. Don't dwell on it though, it just means I have a predilection for mental illness."

"Ha! No wonder we get along! We're both fucked up!" She smiled as she made a few practice swings with her new toy. She mockingly evaded a false attacker, then I believe she stabbed him, twisted her blade, and finally held up something within her fist.

I furrowed my brow and stared at her quizzically. I wondered what the weather in her world is like.

"His balls!" She pointed proudly at the imaginary severed testicles of her victim. She snorted loudly.

"That's a horrible thing to do to someone." I shook my head. "No matter how bad they are."

"Not if he tried to rape you or something," she countered. "Or talked badly about your mom. So not cool."

I shook my head again.

While I stood with the trunk open, I removed a pair of goggles that hung from the actual trunk above me. It read *Binoculars* on the side of them. They were, in all actuality, brass eyewear that extended like a looking glass might have. I placed them over my eyes after removing my own goggles.

They automatically dimmed to accommodate the light. My head swam due to the blurry field of vision at first, they adjusted quickly though. They whirred quietly, tiny gears spun together, like a tiny factory inside the meticulously crafted eyewear. My temples felt every movement.

Adjusting optics.... Scanning retinas... Neural connection made... Khadim Gray... 42 years old. Calibrate. Follow the sights.

I did as it said and followed the small red target that came up across my vision.

Calibration complete.

Everything is done through thoughts. Think and it will apply, Patty's voice said in my head.

I thought about zooming in, it zoomed in. My field of vision became crystal clear. I looked across the desolate land. I thought about the shade being darker, they darkened.

I thought about it snapping a picture, it did. I thought about it opening the picture, it did. Wow. Insanely clever engineering, almost magical.

"What exactly are you doing?" Maddy asked while smoking a cigarette.

I looked at her and thought about it going back to normal vision, it did.

Identify person scrolled in my vision.

"Maddy," I said.

Identity accepted.

She stood outlined in white with a line pointing at her that labeled her as Maddy.

"Yes?" She asked still observing me. "I was speaking to my goggles." I said. "They're neurologically connected. It's weird, but useful."

"Sounds a lot like me." She snickered as she blew smoke through he nostrils.

"They look custom." She commented. "Patty has certainly got some skills."

The lenses followed her as she walked past me.

They switched into a new blue shade. The line that said Maddy on it changed to have a subtext.

It read *Power.*

"What is a Power?" I asked out loud.

Maddy's eyes went wide. She choked on some smoke from her cigarette.

"Like one of those super heroes? Like picking up a car and throwing it, or looking at ladies with X-ray vision?" She smirked, after catching her breath. Her eyes red from the coughing.

"No, on the lens here, it says Maddy, and underneath it, it says Power." I told her.

"Let me see those things." She reached up and pulled them from my head.

I squinted in reaction to having the goggles removed. There was a short dizzy spell as my eyes adjusted to the bright sun, my head started to ache. I put my other goggles back on. They were certainly boring after having the other ones on. But at least they gave me some kind of defense against the brutality of the sun.

Maddy removed her dark lenses and placed the new goggles over her head. She blinked and stared strangely at me.

"These are nuts!" she remarked while waving her hand in front of her face.

She said, "Khadim"

"Ok, Ok, I see." she said nodding. "These say you're Khadim, because I said so, then underneath your name it says Constant." she tilted her eyebrow. "Isn't that what Faul called you?"

"Yes. Wait, it says I'm a Constant?" I asked almost reaching for the glasses.

"Now it says Khadim, Human Constant." She tapped her chin and stared at me grudgingly.

Perhaps it was labeling her as someone with power?

I've never heard that before, but that didn't mean it wasn't possible. I contemplated about what a Power could be, then I saw Maddy freeze.

She watched the horizon intently. She pointed behind me and I turned. "Shavs, we need to bolt."

She handed me the goggles and replaced her own. It calibrated immediately upon replacement. The goggles zoomed in with my thought and showed about twenty miles away. I saw a large faded green truck with the Shavs scarlet logo on the hood. There were probably about five guys packed inside. In the back, a monster of a man with gold and black on his face shouted out directions. He pointed here and there, his enormous maul in his hand, lying flat across the top of the truck. Faul.

When I thought of his name, the goggles labeled him as such.

Faul, Fallen Virtue, Sun

Fallen Virtue? Sun? I don't get these labels. I thought to myself.
Damn things should've come with an instruction manual, at the
very least a damned glossary.

I decided to keep the goggles on, they seemed useful. I looked
inside the trunk and grabbed the.357 and the box of bullets.
Slamming the trunk shut, I jumped in the driver seat, and tossed
the pistol and the bullets to Maddy. They landed in her lap. She sat
there looking shocked at me.

"Load it," I said.

"You mean load it *please*." She sat with her arms across her
chest now.

"Just load it, we might need it." I started the car and she waved
her hand at the radio. She smiled. "Offspring, Bad Habit." Her
head bounced up and down as the music blared. A song about
road rage. Fitting.

She started loading the gun as we drove.

We made it about half a mile before trouble found us again.

We picked up pace as the roadway dropped into a steep
decline. We careened downward, I noticed a graffiti covered eigh-
teen-wheeler parked sideways across the road.

The path filled with its massive girth.

I slammed on the brakes, the car swerved, and we came to a
skidding halt. Of course, a fucking trap. We turned to drive back
and watched as three cars zoomed over the hill. They parked at an
angle to block us in.

We didn't have time for this shit. Faul would be here in
roughly ten minutes. We had to get on the road, I turned the car
off and took the keys.

I unbuckled my seat belt and reached for the door handle.
Maddy freaked out.

"What are you doing?!" She snapped at me with fear in her
eyes. I grabbed the gun from her lap.

"Getting directions," I said as I pulled the handle on the door.

Five men dressed in leather the color of mucus, stood around their cars. They had their rifles and pistols on display. This would go down violently, and with any luck, quickly.

The goggles documented them and informed me they were humans. Very helpful, at least they weren't dragons I guess.

"Give us the car!" One of them shouted from behind his car's hood.

"Yeah!" Another echoed.

"No," I said lowly.

"Excuse me?" One of them had begun to walk towards me with a baseball bat in his hand. Why did so many bad guys have baseball bats? Must've had a sale at Abysm? A horrible cliché really. Their auras were faded, but they had committed atrocities in the past. No reason for mercy.

I let the mouth of the group edge closer to me, he seemed confident he had me. That same sulfur smell from before wafted through the area. Dust whipped around the embankment.

"Give me the car." He snapped again, only a few feet away from me at that point. "Or I'll bash you in the head!" He patted the bat in his hand.

Original.

"Sure thing." I took out the car keys and tossed them down the hill at the passenger door.

I stepped to the side, offering him the road to the car.

He hesitated, his confidence faltered a bit.

"I can go?" I asked, shrugging my shoulders.

"Wait here!" he snapped as he walked down the hill towards the keys. He got near the car and looked to see a long fishnet covered leg sticking out of the car. Maddy had rolled down the window to smoke a cigarette. She had her goggles pulled up over her forehead when she turned her emerald green gaze towards the approaching figure. Maddy grinned suggestively.

The man looked at her in surprise. You didn't need my abilities to see his poor nature, his perversions would control this matter. I could see his aura had stains from sexual assaults on it though. This would work itself out shortly. He walked to the car after he picked up the keys from the ground and placed his hand on the window, leaning over Maddy's leg.

"Do you come with the car?" he asked as he creeped his way further into the window, gawking at her long curvy leg. He placed a hand on her knee.

Maddy didn't let me down. Her machete shot up through his exposed throat. The keys fell from his hands. He reached to hold his throat together. It wouldn't work, I'd seen it a hundred times before. He bled out and slid down to the ground.

Maddy opened the door, knocking him away from the car. His body flopped backwards, and she grabbed the keys from the ground. They tinkled as she shook the blood from them. She got back in the car, and the music came back on.

The other men stood stunned and distracted, busy watching the gory display at the bottom of the hill. One man slapped his hand against his forehead. Taking advantage of their shock, I reached into my pocket and produced the recently acquired magnum from my jacket.

I fired off two shots before they could react. The man on the right who was carrying a rifle of sorts, caught both in the chest. His back exploded open, spraying the car behind him. The impact was enough to throw him into the car. He slumped over, the life already gone from him.

By the time the others realized what had happened, I had already fired another shot. The crudely dressed man turned to come after me, but he was hit in the thigh with the bullet. His leg exploded from underneath him. Spinning in midair, he crashed into the road. His neck probably broke in the process, but I had to look away and get to the other two men before they killed me.

My bullets must have been modified, just like everything else Patty made.

I ran uphill, dodging bullets, certainly a new experience for me. Time slowed as I ducked under the volley and rolled to avoid fatal shots. The fender of the car popped inward as I careened into it for cover, I dared a glance over the bloody hood. The men were just now able to turn and fire at me again, the car quaked from the impact. Adrenaline coursed through my system as I took the offensive.

My target had a pistol leveled at me.

The gun bucked in my hand and the bullet made the short journey into the man's elbow. It had in fact, decided to take the full trip through his right pectoral too. Probably blowing out his lung on the way. His back erupted. His arm fell limp, and he flew backwards out of my vision.

The last guy I needed, had ducked behind the car. I used the opportunity to scuttle around to the back of the car. He poked his head above the hood of the third vehicle and scan the area. While he was doing that, I crept up behind him and placed the barrel to the base of his skull. He whimpered knowing he was caught.

"Two bullets. What's your name?" I asked, clearing my throat.

"T-t-Terry!" he said and my goggles labeled him as *Terry Human.*

That was just neat.

"Good Terry, I'm going to let you live."

"Show me how to get to Ouroboros." I said plainly. His head shook rapidly left and right.

"I don't know how to get there man!" he said.

"Really, I've never been!"

"Now now, calm down. Give me this first." I leaned over and took his gun and his knife off his hip." He didn't budge, aside from the shaking.

"You're a what? Shav?" I guessed. "What?! NO! I'm one of the

Pus Mothers!" He said like a proud fool pointing at his shoulder. I glanced at the patch with a litter of zits on it. Charming.

"Well, you see. Faul is coming this way to try and get me, he kept calling me a Constant. That mean anything to you?" I asked Terry.

"Faul is coming?" His eyes watered up. "No, no, man. No idea what a Constant is! No idea where Ouroboros is either!"

"You're really not much use to me, are you?" I pulled back the hammer on my pistol. He made a noise reminiscent of a rabbit caught in a trap.

"I KNOW SOMEONE!" he yelped. "I KNOW SOMEONE WHO CAN TELL YOU! I'LL TAKE YOU! JUST DON'T SHOOT ME OR LEAVE ME HERE!"

"Well, now we're making progress," I said. "Are your cars automatic or stick?" He raised his eyebrows, sweat dripping down his forehead.

"Just answer the damn question," I snapped.

"A-A-Automatic," he stammered.

Finally, some good news.

"Maddy!" I yelled.

She opened the door with her leg. Leaned out and looked over at me through her goggles.

"Choose one, you're following me." I pointed at the cars. Maddy flashed me the biggest smile I'd ever seen on her face.

CHAPTER 6
THE MAN IN THE SUIT

ACCORDING TO THE goggles, about six minutes had passed. I managed a quick glance behind us, Faul was about fifteen miles back. They followed the same road, more than likely they would lose some time once they got to the blockaded area. They would see the dead bodies and know they were on the right track.

Hopefully this asshole riding shotgun would get us to someone who knew how to get to Ouroboros, so we can meet the lady who was supposed to know what the hell a Constant was. All this bigger purpose bullshit grated my nerves a bit and gnawed at my peace. My patience wore thinner by the minute.

I had bound his hands with some wire I found in the trunk earlier. He bled a bit when I did it, but he'd live. Maddy decided on a blue Honda Civic. Pathetic little thing, but she said it was "sporty". I could care less, if she hit a bump in it, but it would probably get stuck. It confounded me as to why one would lower a car in that landscape. Figured with an apocalypse of sorts you would burn all Civics first chance you had.

I looked at my trembling compadre Terry. "Where are we going and who are we seeing?"

"Jolt knows man! He's fixed shit for those guys, he's good with electricity and stuff. They use lots of that there," he stammered.

His disheveled green hair covered one of his eyes, no wonder he didn't see me in the gunfight.

"Where?" I asked him plainly.

"H-he's a friend. Turn off up here, exit 33b. Stay left." He blew his hair out of his vision.I turned down the dusty road. "You realize that if you lead me into a trap, I'm going to let Maddy cut your balls off and parade them to your friends. She's done it once today already, even though I told her she shouldn't."

His deep brown eyes went wide in horror. "What?! Man, you guys are sick!" I had a fleeting vision hit me unexpectedly.

I saw our viridian haired friend Terry beating a helpless man. He kicked the man in the ribs and in his temple. The rest of his crew did most of the dirty work, but he got his licks in when he could. He chortled gleefully and spit gobs of phlegm on the guy. As the spittle ran down his face, the man cried out that he had given Terry his car keys, and asked why they wouldn't just let him go?! Terry snorted in laughter and answered him by putting a hole in his head with his pistol.

I looked over at him. "Sick is kicking a man in the ribs after he's given you all he had."

Terry looked with wide eyed disbelief shaking his head. "How do you know that?" "I get visions, they're coming more often. It's not a good sign if I get one, typically means you're a world class scumbag." I clicked my tongue. "Scumbags never make it far with me."

He went pale and looked down at his blood-spattered feet. "I've done some stupid shit, but I never killed anyone!"

His aura disagreed with him, stained plain as day, no matter what little thing you've done in the past. It'll be there.

"Why lie to me? Do you think I'm naive to your kind?" I said with my eyes forward to the road.

The vision showed him shooting a man for his wallet.

"You've killed for money."

The vision showed him stabbing a woman in the back for a pack of cigarettes.

"You've killed for smokes."

The vision showed him burning a store down to the ground with people tied up inside. Their screams drowned out by the flames.

"You've killed for food."

He sat silently staring at his feet with his head lulling.

"Are you a psychic or something man? How do you know this stuff?" He visibly shuddered as he looked at me.

"Heh, I'm no psychic." I smirked at him remembering when Maddy asked me something similar. "I'm still learning who I am. People keep calling me names, showing me things I don't understand, and directing me to places to go and find myself." I stared at the roadway blankly.

"I just happen to keep running into assholes like you along the way."

He turned his head back towards the floorboards.

The rest of the trip was silent except for a few turns into an abandoned neighborhood. Busted up houses and windows, swaying trees, and knocked over fences. A pack of dogs wandered aimlessly. However, right in the middle of it all stood a pristine house. A bright shining light of life, amidst the rotting carcass of the Outlands. Like a predator standing proudly amongst the scattered remains of its prey.

A huge oak fence surrounded thick green hedges, the grasses a rich green and perfectly trimmed. This meant it had to be watered daily. On the gate, I saw a big double J in polished golden letters, glinting in the sunlight.

Are you kidding me. Could you have not made more of a beacon out of yourself?

"Jolt's I presume," I stated, eyeballing Terry.

"Yes. Let me out and I'll put you in contact with him." He bobbed his head up and down.

I looked him over, I shook my head. "Nah." "I'll pull up to the gate and you can ring the doorbell, and we can chat as a group. Real friendly like," I said.

We drove up to the front and got out, an arrow on a panel said Press Me in golden letters. I nodded to my buddy Terry and he rang the doorbell with his knuckle.

The doorbell sang out merrily across a finely tuned speaker system. Clearly subtlety is not something this Jolt cared about. The tinny melody echoed out across the dead world around us to die away in the distance.

Maddy sat back in her car. She watched from afar and kept an eye out for Faul. Since we got off the freeway, there could be a slim chance they might overlook us. This neighborhood wasn't far from the freeway, but vague enough to camouflage us. Hopefully. That house though? I had my doubts they'd miss it. The panel whirred and flipped over. I spotted a monitor on the other side and watched as it flickered on. A sharply dressed man with a slick pompadour styled high appeared on the screen and grinned widely. The camera tilted downwards on his end, giving his head a sloping appearance.

"Terry, I see you have come unannounced to my home, which I presume is due to some mild level of insistence." he said with a smooth rich tone. "Will the man beside you kill you if I don't let you in? Also, what is this in regard to, sir? I don't owe you money, do I? Because I assure you I can pay any debts if that's the case. Hmmhmm."

Terry spoke next. "Look man, he wants to go to Ouroboros. I told him you could help since you've worked there or whatever." I stepped into the camera's view. "You give me a map or a detailed explanation, I'll leave you and Terry here alone."

The man in the monitor's eyebrows creased upwards and his smile grew wider. "Oh, on the contrary," he said politely with a grin. "I'd much rather enjoy helping someone of your, qualifi-cations. You clearly know how to get what you want." "You can release Terry. He knows his way out," he said. "Please, have your young lady give the car back to Terry. He needs to leave *now*. She can come inside too."

I let go of Terry's shoulder as I signaled to Maddy to pull up. She did so and looked at me through the window with concern in her eyes. I motioned for her to get out. She visibly sighed and climbed out of the car, drudging over with pouty steps.

"What?" she said with an apprehensive look on her face, even though she already knew what I wanted.

"Give him the car," I told her.

She groaned. "Seriously? I get to drive and you're going to take it away from me? Just like that? That's some bullshit Khadim. Why does this asshole get to leave anyways?" She pointed at him and gave him an accusatory glance like an older sister blaming her younger brother for something.

"Sir, if you cannot accommodate me, I shan't be able to accommodate you." The man on the camera screen smiled again. His teeth shown wide on the monitor. "Time, is of the essence."

Maddy rolled her green eyes with obvious disdain. "You're too damned trusting." She chided me.

My goggles didn't register anything for Jolt. I imagined it was because he was behind a monitor. After Maddy got out of the car, she turned around and violently stabbed the front seat with her machete. The innards of the seat spilled out onto the floorboard.

"Asshole," she said under her breath, then stopped him.

"Whoa there buddy," she said with a mischievous grin on her face. "Let me get that wire for you." She pointed at his wrists.

He eyed her apprehensively and shook his hands at her.

"No, that's ok."

"No! I insist." She grabbed his wrists and pulled outwardly in front of him. She didn't wait for his permission.

"Hold em' real steady now." Her eyes widened as she steadied her aim.

She closed her eyes and raised the machete skyward.

"Oh God no!" Terry spouted as the blade arced downward and sliced clean through the tangle of wires.

Clearly shock had not registered in Terry because he looked surprised to be alive. Genuinely relieved to see the wires were completely cleaved off him. It wasn't until he noticed she had sliced the tip of his right pinky off. There it wobbled on the ground next to the wire. His eyes went wide, realization had finally hit him.

"My finger!" He shrieked and went pale as he grabbed his sputtering digit.

Maddy wiped the bloody machete off on the screaming man's jacket. She then slid it back in the holster and came over to me while Terry scrounged for the knuckle on his pinky.

"Now we can go in." She tilted her head and grinned sweetly. I shook my head.

The gate opened to reveal a large statue of a gorilla. It towered over Maddy and me. The gorilla stood in a full suit. Nothing relevant, just a bizarre piece of artwork to be sitting out like this. It looked almost lifelike. Jolt certainly seemed a tad eccentric.

We rushed around to the front door where Jolt stood, a man with an obvious style. His dark suit hugged his lithe frame perfectly, his tan face smooth and completely hairless. On his head, each strand of his perfect black hair stood in solidarity with one another, and his smile oozed with charisma. Black glasses hid his eyes and the rest of his features.

My goggles finally read, *Johnny Jolt, Fallen Virtue, Storm.*

Again, the words were cryptic and scattered to say the least. Faul is a Fallen Virtue too, but these two didn't seem to be the same, at least not at first glance or by outward appearance. Faul's also said Sun and Jolt's says Storm. Were they elements?

Terry mentioned Jolt knew electricity. Could it be a new lingo for this society? An electrician might work with storms? I had no clue, this was all just guesswork.

"Hey you kids." Our sharply dressed host said.

"Ouroboros huh? That sure is swell, I think that place could use some excitement like you two." He smiled and wobbled his head.

"Where are my manners, come in, come in. I'm Johnny Jolt." He smiled widely and bowed deeply. "Electric wizard." He snapped his fingers and pointed at us.

"You kids do realize that you have Faul on your tail, right?" He walked us inside and pointed to some monitors with video of the truck on the wall. "But, since I dig you two so much, I sent Terry as a distraction." He grinned that wide grin of his. "That Faul is a bloodhound, he'll sniff you out sooner or later, this however..." he picked up a remote and changed all monitors to one.

A feed of Terry driving in the Civic to get on the freeway. Turned out it was the perfect amount of time for Faul to catch up to him at the cross street. They all got out and pulled Terry from his car.

Maddy chortled loudly. "What an asshole."

"No doubt Terry will tell him everything he knows about you, and your journey. He'll probably come here next, but he cannot enter here. It's sacred ground baby!" He leaned back with both heels together and thrust his chest up and out. "That means it's mine, and not his." He pulled his glasses down to expose yellow eyes, he wiggled his eyebrows in unison.

"You're one of the thirteen?" Maddy said.

Jolt fell into another scraping bow, his gloved right hand swung like a pendulum into an arc and back to his chest. "Something like that." He winked and put his glasses back on.

"Don't worry. I'm not some hellbent biker bent on taking over towns for knick-knacks." He tutted wagging a finger and clicked his tongue. "I'm into helping folks out." He smiled. "To quote a poet from times before, 'I'm not a businessman, I'm a business, man.'"

"So, you have another five minutes. I can protect this area, but not you. Dig?" He grinned.

"Let's just say that I can…" he looked at me raising his eyebrows.

"Who made those peepers?" He leaned over to see the goggles. I reached up and touched them. "Patty, I think."

"That old fox is still kicking huh? That's marvelous." He rubbed his hands together nervously.

"Well, look. Let me get a hold of those peepers and I'll fix you up with a location." He extended his silky golden glove.

I took off the goggles and handed them to Jolt. He took them from my hands eagerly, and made his way into a small office. The walls were littered with monitors, hundreds of them, a tad overkill if you'd asked me. This guy was a bit of a voyeur.

He sat in a red velvet chair that rolled on golden wheels. He pulled out a plug from the arm of it, connecting it into the goggles. Poking at some imaginary buttons in front of him, he stabbed the air for a moment, then wiggled his finger in a circle. I guessed his sunglasses had a monitor. "And that's that." He smiled. "Double data transfer. I got all that you've seen, and you get the way to Ouroboros."

"Groovy," he said and handed the goggles back to me. I watched as he released the wire and it snapped back into the arm of the chair. He stood up and placed his hand on my back and guided me out the door.

"Better be on your way now…" he smiled. "All with three and a half minutes to spare." He waved as he herded us out the front door.

As we were ushered outside, we both stood dazed. I'm not sure what all had just happened, but it seemed easy enough. Probably too much so.

We walked to the car, and on the way, I swear I saw that gorilla statue move. Getting back on the road seemed like my only path to normality, provided we manage to avoid the psychopath in the truck.

Jolt's silky tones replaced Patty's voice in my googles. "Hello there beautiful! It's time to go to Ouroboros! The word scrolled past in bold white letters. Just follow the dotted line! I even made an escape route as to avoid that pesky hammer-wielding Faul!" Jolt's giggle echoed through my head.

I thought to myself, *Can you hear me Jolt?*

"Of course I can. You think that a being with my importance, couldn't surpass Patty's defenses? I'm merely interested in the ride. I've got to be honest, this is one sweet car! Patty being who she is though, does not surprise me one bit. No sir!"

I'm not sure what I thought about Jolt being in my head. Like that, he responded.

"Don't worry baby! I can't get to those memories or anything. Just what you're thinking every second you have these goggles on. Don't worry, I don't take things personally. Life is just a good ol' game to play. There are winners and there are losers. Let's try to make you win ok? Alright!" I prepared myself for a rough ride to Ouroboros. Having someone in my head, reading my thoughts for who knows how long? Shoot me.

It had only been a few miles, but Jolt let me know that Faul had showed up.

"He should stop here and try to find some information. Possibly attempt to kill me, you know? The norm," Jolt said through the glasses. "I'll only be a momentary distraction though."

"Don't sweat it though. He can't do squat to the J-man." He said reassuringly.

The GPS within the glasses worked spectacularly. A line appeared in front of me, guiding my every move. Similar to the crap that the old phone companies used to put out, but far more three dimensional and intuitive. "Head right at Smith street in five hundred feet," Jolt's automated voice said.

I turned Pearl to the right and we continued along the road until we came up on the freeway. "Turn left onto Ten West." I did.

Maddy sat there looking troubled. She bit her nails fervently. Something troubled her right now.

"What's the matter?" I asked.

She nibbled on her thumbnail and squinted her eyes doubtfully at me. "What's Jolt's deal? He gets something out of this and I don't see what it is," She said after spitting out a freshly bitten nail.

"Jolt, what are you getting out of this?" I asked out loud.

My left eye flickered and a feed with Jolt in it appeared. He had his head leaned forward with that huge charismatic grin of his showing.

"Baby look, I'm just in the market for information. You can provide information. It'll become clearer once you get to Ouroboros." he paused. "You're going to seek Solace right?"

"Yes, how did you know that?" I asked him.

"We Virtues just know. Which is bad for you because Faul knows too. Which is bad for the soul, brother!" he said.

"What is a virtue?" I asked him. Hoping I'd get a straight answer.

No such luck.

"A title and nothing more. One that we had to come upon on our own time. You're here like I was here man," he said. "By the way, Faul didn't stay here long cuz' he digs those rules like I said." He lowered his glasses showing his luminescent yellow eyes. "You've got to hurry. That truck is much faster than it looks."

I gazed up into the rear-view mirror and sure enough, I could see the oversized Faul clearly, and unfortunately, I didn't have to zoom in to do so. He had his maul hoisted skyward and pointed towards us.

I punched the accelerator and Pearl roared into full throttle.

Flames erupted out of the blower. It growled and shook the car. The world became a blur as I followed the line on the pavement. My knuckles ran white as I gripped the wheel for dear life.

Debris cluttered the three-lane highway. Dead, abandoned cars littered the roadway. Most had been cleared out, but some still took up full lanes.

I swerved past a red car that had been flipped sideways on the road. Looking back, I saw Faul standing in the back of that truck with both hands held onto the roof. He seemed to have a faint glow to him. The exhaust of his truck bellowed fire. It left a long smoke trail behind it. When I turned back towards the road ahead, it was already too late.

CHAPTER 7
TERRA

THE KID CAME from nowhere. He stood in the middle of the road and stared fearlessly at us. He stood between the only gap in the freeway and two overturned cars. My ankle twisted as I hammered on my brakes. The stubborn car fought me for every inch. The wheel's protestations were too much for me. It spun out of my grasp. We fishtailed sideways and whipped into a full tilt spin. Smashing through some debris in the road, the car began to tumble. This was when I became thankful for the roll cage in Pearl.

I stared through the front windshield as the world flipped and spun out of control. I glanced over at Maddy and saw that blood streamed from her ears. Her eyes were closed tightly and she had a grimace on her face. She hung suspended in the air by her seat belt as gravity took over again. I wondered if she would survive this crash.

The car quaked and our bodies caromed in a new direction as we smashed into one of the other cars on the highway. Glass exploded around us. Tiny shards danced midair like glitter. Patiently they waited to fall and settle deep into our skin. My head careened off of the steering wheel. Blood plastered the inside of my front windshield. The rest of the crimson droplets joined the glass in the suspended ballet above us.

My left wrist smashed against the dashboard and it snapped my hand at an unfamiliar angle. My arm buckled under my weight as well, my elbow ached. Lightning hot pain arced up my arm and back down my spinal column. Maddy's limp body snapped back and forth violently while somehow staying latched into her seat.

Maddy's chest heaved, it was raw and bloody from the tightness of the restricting seatbelt. It amazed me how the world slowed down in these situations. Every detail so clear and concise to me. Then reality came crashing back in.

The world came to a roaring halt. My head swam and I could barely keep my eyes open. Maddy laid still, slumped over in her seat. We were turned sideways looking out towards the highway. In my daze, I saw Faul rapidly close the distance. It wouldn't be the crash that killed me, it would be the oversized menace who ended my brief stint in this crazy world.

Then the car shifted ever so slowly and evened itself with the horizon. We plateaued and came to rest on the highway. I credited my possible concussion with the current state of movement.

A small kid, probably in his early teens stood and considered the passenger side window of Pearl. His cinnamon colored skin shone with a thick membrane of sweat. His tightly cropped hair enhanced his large hazel eyes. We made eye contact briefly and he said something, not to me, but to himself.

"Hello serendipity." Came the whisper, as he turned his gaze back to the highway and the oncoming truck.

He extended his arm and we slid backwards. As we moved, I saw Faul's truck plow directly into the kid, a horn roared loudly. An explosion rang out and the impact shook us. The blaring horn went silent, and I watched the vehicle wrap itself around the kid in an instant.

The handful of men in the back of the truck launched like projectiles in different directions. They would not be troubling us any longer. I gaped in astonishment as the kid hoisted a two-ton truck over his head. What impressed me even more was the fact that Faul had held on through the entire crash.

Terra turned the truck onto its side and Faul leapt from the vehicle and rolled to the side. His maul sparked against the pavement, cratering the concrete as he went. His grip never wavered. Behind him, the truck folded in upon itself as the earth snaked around it and dragged it deep, along with the remaining unconscious men, far underground.

Faul's seven foot frame rose from the ground and pointed his enormous weapon at the chest of the kid.

"Move Terra, this is your only warning. The Constant is mine." Faul glowered as he stared down his nose at him.

He hoisted his maul overhead and brought it crashing into the ground in front of the kid. The ground erupted and flames jetted from around the weapon. Rocks and debris kicked up through the air. The kid stood his ground, brushed the debris aside with a gesture, and locked eyes with Faul.

They looked like David and Goliath. I only hoped that it would turn out the same way.

A brief moment of silence passed between them. The two warriors stared one another down.

The ground shook as the kid, Terra, made the first move and ran towards the behemoth in front of him.

Maddy stirred momentarily where she laid, her skin looked paper white. I nudged her and tried to get her seat belt off.

"Maddy if you're still with me get up, we have to go," I said as the seat belt unlatched and she slumped into my arms.

"Constant." I heard in my head. I had forgotten about my glasses entirely. "You ok kiddo?" Jolt implored.

I didn't have time to talk to him. I had to get out of there. According to the GPS, we were still a multitude of miles away from the city of Ouroboros. Who knew exactly where we were? We couldn't have made it that far.

"Maddy is alive, just get to the side. Stand your ground or Faul will keep coming after you. Cripple him," he said. "but don't kill him, it's important he lives!"

My wrist throbbed and sat there misshapen. Where my arm had been fractured, the bone protruded through the skin. At least it had moments ago when I saw it all happen, it had mended itself. My skin knitted itself back together right in front of me. The bone ached as it reset. I didn't know why or how, but I guessed it was probably how I survived my time in that basement.

My wrist healed on the inside and I could feel the nerves coming back. It seemed the more I noticed it, the better it healed. So, I concentrated on my wrist, and it seemed I'd be able to snap my fingers again in no time. My body didn't feel like it had even been in an accident moments ago.

Another concussive explosion, I looked back to the fight to see Faul slamming his maul into the ground again at Terra. The teenager seemed tough. He gestured, and the rubble that came at him flew sideways as he charged at Faul fearlessly.

I had to help him. Maddy could wait in the car.

How could this kid handle a monster like Faul on his own? Even IF he had just crushed a car with his body, the odds were stacked against him.

I sat up in my seat and grabbed the door handle, it clicked uselessly. I leaned back and put my legs into it. It took a few solid kicks, but it wailed loudly in disapproval as it swung outward. I stood up, and watched the two super humans doing battle. The glasses labeled the kid, *Terra Virtue Earth*. He battled against the immense Faul.

I watched as the giant swung his maul sideways into the ribs of Terra. The kid crumpled sideways as the blow collapsed his side. His eyes went wide in shock, his teeth ground against one another. He grimaced in agony.

Terra had just stopped a truck with his body alone, but the maul had landed solidly. His side smoldered as the maul came away from him, the skin stuck and smoked. The smell of burning flesh wafted through the air.

Faul hefted the maul over his head and dropped it down onto Terra's leg like the massive weapon weighed nothing. His knee splintered under the weight. A smoking piece of meat remained on the ground in the place of the kid's leg. Terra screamed in agony, his leg burned in the white hot sun. He grabbed at his thigh and tried to slide back and away.

Before Faul could bring his hammer up a second time, the ground in front of Terra shot up and stuck through Faul's chest. A feint, I was impressed by this maneuver. The giant looked down at the large piece of earth covered in fresh blood. He brought his forearm down on it and crashed through it. He pulled the stone spear from his chest and flung it on the ground, growling at Terra in blind rage.

As Faul looked up, he gnashed his teeth and snarled at Terra. Before he could advance, another pillar of earth shot through the other side of his chest. Faul howled in pain. The maul clanged off the ground as he dropped it to grab the earth protruding through his torso. Faul groaned as he struggled to remove that one.

Using his legs as leverage, he heaved, the ground underfoot gave way as well. He drove a now glowing fist into the stone, it refused to give. He wailed on the cone over and over until it started to visibly crack.

Terra fell to his back and rolled to look at me pleadingly. "A little help?"

I looked over at Faul and his skin began to undulate heat. Flames poured over his body in waves and the earth in his chest began to smoke as he slammed his fists into it, over and over.

That acrid odor of sulfur soured the air. Terra tried standing up, but it didn't work. His leg was in shambles. Terra turned his attention back to Faul and worked the earth to strengthen the spike, his face was a mask of pain and determination.

There on the ground behind Faul, laid my opportunity. I ran behind the raging bastard and scooped up his maul. It burned white hot; My hands seared under the heat, yet I felt no pain at that moment, possibly all the nerves in my hands had just been burned out. I struggled to lift it. The damn thing must have weighed fifty pounds.

With concentrated effort, I heaved it high over my head and crashed it down the center of his shoulder blades. He sagged deeper onto the spear, growling in pain as he realized my presence there.

The earth in his chest erupted further out of his back, sizzling as it shifted through his skin. The waves of flames that gusted from his body grew wider and longer, they licked at my frame. I drew the hammer overhead again and battered it down harder, envisioning a circus game, where you're trying to hit the bell in a show of strength. Bones broke under the hammer's blow. His right arm hung limply at his side.

Further the spike of earth shifted through Faul. The heatwave raged, the searing waves forcing me backward. My flesh burned under my leather jacket. The leather itself started to stink and the metal zippers glowed bright from the intense heat, my hands ached and went numb. I felt light headed in this onslaught. Terra redoubled his efforts, shifting on his side making gestures through the air again at Faul. The earth twisted around Faul and throughout his body.

Faul burned brightly as he shouted.

"I will kill you Constant, like the ones before you. I will kill you, and every other Constant who rises after you." He bellowed through the pain, glowing ever brighter.

The unbearable heat grew in its intensity. Forced to move back as my jacket ignited under the sweltering temperature. I patted the jacket down.

My skin thickened, protecting me from the heat. My knuckles swelled like boxing gloves. My body went into overdrive.

I watched as the earth swallowed up Faul to his neck, a slow painful suffocation. The ground burned and melted, inching its way over his body. I couldn't watch directly any longer. Faul burned as a living sun in the middle of the freeway. The world smelled of fire, sulfur stifled my senses. My eyes watered and ran down my face, only to evaporate moments later.

I grasped the maul in both hands with the head low to the ground behind me and charged in with the maul drawn back as I ran. My body ached, I couldn't see, and the world was going to burn me to ashes. The water in my body was being sapped from me, I only had moments to end this. The maul cooked right through my gloves and into my hands, my own flesh smoked. It felt as if the gates of hell had opened its maw and swallowed me whole. Truly the most pain I had ever felt, but honestly, I would be chased no longer. I would endure the pain.

Jolt shouted something into my head, a distant sound in the background. I disregarded him as I plummeted into Hades head first.

I twisted the maul back over my head like I was going to drive a golf ball a thousand yards. As the pendulum swung and my arms shook from the weight of the maul, I grinned.

The hit connected and Faul's neck snapped cleanly. His jaw separated from the lower half of his face and his head spun backwards. I heard a prominent *CRACK!* Gore was all that remained below his cheeks.

I panted as I stood over him.

It seemed that someone turned the power off. The heat dissipated immediately and Faul's body lay there stuck in the ground. His jaw spun in the wind, a dangling mess attached by a thread of skin. His eyes that had turned so dark black, turned solid white.

The ground around him glistened, the sand and stones in the ground had turned into glass from the immense heat. All around us the light reflected from above, it twinkled in the sunlight. A haunting beauty, in a place of death and destruction.

An overwhelming sense of power surged throughout my body.

My eyes rolled back in my head, my muscles swelled and flesh emanated. The maul felt lighter in my grasp, the heat outside seemed suddenly bearable. I could see clearly and the sun no longer phased my eyesight. I looked at my hands where they smoldered moments ago. They had become spotless, I looked and felt younger.

Jolt broke the silence. "Holy shit, I can't believe you killed him. Not good, that is not good my man." Terra crawled over to me. During the fight he must have splinted his leg with the earth. He stood up, and leaned on my shoulder to support himself. He grabbed onto me for balance. His frame so much smaller than mine.

"Solace sent me to find you, she needs to talk to you," he said through a grimace, his clothes were still smoking from the heat.I looked at him. Jolt chimed in his two cents.

"Terra is no punk man. He's going to give you direct access, sans bullshit from Ouroboros." I looked back at Pearl, the driver side door agape from where I left it earlier.

"I've got to take her," I said. The car remained in good shape even after the crash. The windows were smashed up and the sides were busted in, but the tires and engine seemed to be just fine. I looked at the ground behind the car, it protruded out and rested against the car as a cushion.

It had just occurred to me that Terra had caught the car as we flipped in the air. Evident by the hand prints embedded in the passenger side door. His fingers had gone through it and the earth had come up and stabilized the vehicle. How the hell did this happen? I scratched the new flesh on my hands, it itched. This world constantly surprised me.

"I'm sorry it had to be this way," Terra said as he looked at Maddy in the car. "I didn't mean to cause the accident, I didn't think I could catch you if you got past, and I worried Faul would get to you first. I panicked."

I gave Terra a piercing look.

"If Maddy dies. I will kill you for it, if she lives, you'll be fine," I said plainly. The girl had grown on me; she was kind of my guardian in a way.

"I'll take you to Solace, she can tell you everything," he said. "Your friend will be ok, I promise."

"We need to take your car Constant; I don't have one. Take the maul too," he gestured to the dangling weapon in my hands. "it may come in handy." I had forgotten I even held onto it. I shook Faul's remains from it, they sizzled as they hit the ground. I slung it over my shoulder. The remaining heat that resonated from it didn't bother me anymore.

We moved Maddy to the backseat and strapped her in. She breathed sporadically. I worried she wouldn't make it, and I'd have to live up to my promise and in fact kill Terra. Even though I doubted I could do that.

I walked over to the driver's side and Terra climbed into the passenger side. The earth around the vehicle flattened out around us. "Really sorry about the car again. I didn't really plan this out too much." He apologized.

I turned the key in the ignition and Pearl roared back to life. Grateful that she was built so damned tough, we were almost ready to take off.

First, I sat Maddy up and propped her against the side so she could be comfortable. She was covered in blood on her chest and neck. The blood from her ears and the damage from the seatbelt had made a mess of her. She breathed heavily still, I hoped she would be ok.

As we set out, we had no problems, especially with Faul being absent from the equation. His maul rested in the backseat on the floorboard.

Terra sat quietly as we drove, he grimaced occasionally from pain. About an hour into the drive, I heard a brief pop and a groan from his leg, as he set his bones using the earth around it. I'd never seen such a thing done before, but I figured after that last fight I would just let it be. I probably wouldn't be too talkative either. Teens could always be a little awkward.

My black leather had faded to a dull gray, and a lot of it had burned away due to the immense heat from Faul. I felt invigorated from the encounter, like I'd drank a cup of lightning. My senses and vision were so much sharper. I felt as if I could take on anyone. I hoped it would last.

So, let's just cover our bases quickly. These people who can control elements of sorts are called Virtues. Jolt has a hold of electricity, hence his penchant for electronics. Like, he can speak directly with them. Terra which I think means Earth anyways, has control of it. Literally changing the shape and mass of earth, and I'm guessing he does it with his thoughts? Faul, clearly *had* the sun's ability. Able to shift the very heat and light within himself, so much that he made flames pour from his body. If it were not for meeting up with Terra, he would have overwhelmed me for certain. My unconscious companion Maddy was a Power, I'm still not sure what that was. So far, she talked a lot and picked at herself. Pretty sure that didn't define a Power.

That just left me, the Constant. The thing that no one could explain, or would explain, except for this Solace person apparently. I had some guesses, but I would save them for this woman. I had more questions than anything. Why could I heal myself? How far did it go? Am I the only one? How could I withstand Faul's heat, hot enough to turn sand to glass, but a mere annoyance to me. Why had Jolt worried about me killing Faul? What's Jolt's endgame in this? Just too many things to worry about right now.

I didn't like thinking about it. It encroached on my peace, like a thorn in my foot, every step reminding me it's there. I would pull it out if I could get a handle on it, but it stuck in deep, tormenting me.

CHAPTER 8
OUR FIRST GLIMPSE

JUST LIKE A wall where the sun had run its course, the darkness loomed ahead. Never a welcome sight for me, it reminded me of the basement, and that similar cadence of dripping in my head. I would never let that happen again.

We were still miles out, but the city started to show over the horizon. It was immense, no, colossal? Immeasurable? None of these words would do it justice, it was just really fucking big.

As I looked up, I could only see the bottom of the rotating dish. When we had crested underneath it, I don't know. It spanned our entire view as we went.

The color of the dish a dark pewter and it cast a glaring reflection from the white sun. The top came to a point many miles above us, lost amongst the clouds. It reminded me of the Eiffel Tower, but a hundred times larger. Except at the peak of the tower it had a large spinning dish around it that looked like it moved.

Holy shit, it made sense now. It spun to simulate day and night. Incredible, but I couldn't fathom the cost of something like that, or the sheer amount of materials it took to make it. The technology that went into that undertaking would have been staggering. To see it from this far away, I could only imagine what it might look like up close. It had to be breathtaking.

"Holy shit." I exhaled unintentionally.

Terra turned and looked at my astonishment.

"Yeah," Terra said after his long silence. "I have the same reaction every time, and I've lived there for the past twenty years." He looked at the structure with what might have been an artist's appreciation. "You forget what it looks like from the outside when you're in there."

I cocked my head to the side when he mentioned his time there.

"Twenty years? You don't look a day older than fourteen." He sighed and his shoulders sagged. "I wish I could age, it would definitely make it less creepy for the people I tried to flirt with." He gave a sad smile and exhaled sharply through his nose. "Teenagers aren't exactly the most interesting lot, believe me, I've been one since as far back as I can remember."

His aura glowed orange, he had the cleanest soul I'd seen since being released. A deep purple line emanated on the inner ring near him, sadness. Perhaps something to do with his eternal youth? I didn't know him, but from what I'd seen so far, he longed for something else. He looked up at me with his hazel eyes.

I considered his sadness and wondered to myself what it might have been like living as a permanent teenager. The acne alone would make it hell. Much less being in an endless state of puberty.

"We're going to have to find a place to rest soon." I told him.

"I don't really need much sleep, and I don't think you do either," he said.

Couldn't argue with him about that. I hadn't felt weary since I woke up on the gurney. I wasn't even sure I'd slept at all in that hell hole they found me in. I looked at Maddy, totally out cold, but her breathing had evened out. Her shirt lay in tatters across her chest from the seatbelt. The blood from her chest had dried, giving it the look of an old worn out bandage that desperately needed changing.

"We don't, but she does." I nodded at our unconscious companion.

"What's her story?" Terra asked me as he turned and looked at her.

"No clue, met her when I got released," I said.

The wind roared past as we sped through the wasteland without windows, the tangy iron smell of blood still prevalent from the wreck. I kept the radio off as we spoke over the noise.

"What do you mean you were released, were you kidnapped?" He turned and looked at me with a furrowed brow.

"I honestly couldn't give you the details on that either. I can vividly see other people's memories, but not my own. When I am able to recall something, it just hits me out of nowhere. Like my name, Khadim, I didn't remember it when prompted to give it, and then boom! It was there when I needed it," I explained.

"Khadim huh? I like that better than Constant."

"Me too, it is much more becoming," said Jolt in my head.

I'd completely forgotten about him.

"My real name is Terrance, but my mom always called me Terra for short, I think she wanted a girl." He smiled and shrugged.

A normal conversation would be welcome about now. Before that could happen though, I had something to ask Jolt about.

"Jolt, why are you so upset that Faul is dead?" I asked for clarification.

Terra furrowed his brows briefly cast a glance my way, but didn't ask any questions.

Jolt replied in typical Jolt fashion.

"Not my place, guy. Not my place. I'm just here to help you along your way, OK!" He deflected in his normal jovial tone.

Of course. I thought.

"I hate all this mystery bullshit. What is a Constant?" I asked them both out loud. I turned to Terra and stared accusingly at him for a second.

Jolt remained silent, while Terra looked at me and appeared to be about to offer something, then stopped. That just pissed me off.

"On top of that, what the hell is a Virtue?!"

Again, nothing.

Terra fidgeted in his seat, looking for literally anything to focus on aside from me. He glanced at me and probably answered out of sheer guilt.

"Look man." Terra started, "We're on your side. We just can't give you the proper education you're asking for right now. It's not our place."

Jolt seeing his out in this, chimed in his support.

"Terra's speaking truth man!" Terra looked at my goggles. He tilted his head and looked at the sides.

"May I?" He gestured with his hands.

This had become commonplace with these things, people loved inspecting them.

Once my vision become better acclimated to the light, I could drive without them, it would be nice to have Jolt out of my head too. I took the goggles off and handed them to Terra.

He took them from my hands and chuckled.

"You know the lady who made these?" he asked me with an eyebrow up.

"Patty?" I said."That's the one," he said smiling. "She's the lady who designed Ouroboros and the massive spinning tower, Yggdrasil. She's quite possibly the most amazing engineer the world has seen." He beamed, then suddenly, that somber look showed up on his face again."She left though when her partner died. Pearl helped her design and build Ouroboros, and one day while working on the building, she slipped on some loose stone and fell to her death. A two hundred story fall has an abrupt end." He motioned a fall with his hand.

"Just awful, I remember Patty losing it, she locked herself up in her room. Within a week, she was gone. The worst part is they never found her girlfriend's body, she fell into the dark. Demons probably took her over."

He paused while I absorbed the story.

"No chance she survived?" I asked.

"Doubtful, that's a two-thousand-foot drop. Can't imagine any way she didn't look like hamburger helper at the end of that trip." He countered with a grin.

"Gross, and that's terrible. You know, that's what the car is called. Pearl." I nodded at the vehicle we sat inside of.

It now made sense why she would want it back so badly. Aside from being an amazing vehicular creation, it was tied to her partner. She must have had big plans for me if she just handed the keys over so easily.

"Why did she leave Ouroboros?" I asked Terra.

He handed the goggles back to me, and I placed them back on my head.

"I dunno, I would imagine she didn't want to run into the demon version of the love of her life." He sighed sharply. "I don't know what I would do in that situation. If you think about someone you loved, survived all the odds with, and overcame every obstacle in your path." He shook his head. "Could you kill that person if they showed up as a demon?"

I shook my head sideways.

"I couldn't either. I would want to die to be with them. It's too much for anyone," Terra said.

He looked forward toward the road. "I would have left too." He surmised aloud.

We drove for another few hours on the freeway, though it didn't feel like we were getting anywhere closer to Ouroboros, or the massive spinning building. The city just loomed larger, as we coasted along the path.

I reluctantly placed the goggles back on my head.

"Jolt, you there?" I asked.

"ALWAYS!" He said from the screen that popped up in my vision. He stood there with that sloping view. He looked so ominous there, like a villain, rubbing his hands, plotting my death. If it wasn't for his personality, and Terra's aura, I would wonder about him.

"How much further?" I asked Jolt.

"Well, we have several paths we could take, I'm currently taking you as the ol' crow flies. The fastest, dig? It's not the safest route, but it IS the most direct. I have, NO DOUBT, you'll be fine."

This place is enormous, but it houses only a single entrance at the base. All that concrete and a single doorway to get in, it's the safest spot in the dark. As you can imagine, it is also the most heavily fortified. We're talking biblical here. There are four enormous walls surrounding the entirety of the area, each one a staggering 216 feet thick, the walls are fourteen hundred miles around, three gates per wall, and each made of a single pearl. It's fucking huuuuuugggge."

"Great," I said. "Now let me clarify. How many miles away is it?"

"Cool it Constant, you're new blood." Jolt's voice reverberated in my ears. "Learn the land as we go, appreciate those fine peepers you got from Patty." He smarted. "Ouroboros is the city within the walls my man, once inside, you'll have to make your way to Yggdrasil, the home of the wealthiest and most noble of families. I even have an apartment there." He chuckled. "My digs are always the brightest."

I pictured rooms with gigantic blinking neon signs that said Jolt in capital letters all over the apartment, maybe some gorillas in suits doing dishes and taking out the trash. I tried to guide the conversation back to the point.

"Miles, that's all I'm asking." I almost stopped the car.

"Five hundred and sixty-five miles, sixty-five of which are in the dark," he said.

"Finally...Five hundred and sixty-five miles til we're there, sixty-five in the dark," I repeated for Terra to hear.

"That sixty-five is going to feel like two hundred," He said with a look of concern. "At least they don't know we're coming yet, and it's a fast car."

"Now, why is this going to be such a tall task? I'm guessing you had to have driven to come find me, you seem to make it through just fine."

How else would he have gotten to me?

"I got teleported," he said nonchalantly as though teleportation was a normal thing to discuss within the confines of the real world.

Great, now people could teleport.

"Teleportation is a thing now huh?" I asked with wide eyes staring towards the road.

"Well, the teleportation only works for us. It's a one-way trip too. Probably not what you think either, science caused the teleportation, not magic or mutant powers like out of a comic book." He explained. "Solace is the one who owns the portal."

"Patty's design?" I guessed.

"Pearl's actually, more of the mad scientist variety than her counterpart. Patty just built it with her." Terra played with some sand that he had collected from the open window. "It's still technically experimental because the only people teleported have been Jolt and I."

I looked through the goggles and searched for shelter along the road, I felt like I had pushed Maddy far enough without a break. She slept soundly, but I wanted to make sure that she didn't have a fever or anything of that nature. I scanned the road ahead for any kind of safe place to stop, the goggles accommodated my thoughts and plotted a path to the nearest haven. The goggles flashed the words Deep Diner, a place just up ahead.

It would have to do.

CHAPTER 9
THE DEEP DINER

THE SUN IN the sky burned brightly, you could physically see the heat in the car wavering in front of us. Even after the energy boost from Faul's death, I had sweat leaking out of every pore. Terra seemed to be able to move the muscles in his leg again, though the earth around it had not shifted at all.

We pulled up to the side of a rusting sign that read DEEP DINER in fresh black spray paint. There may have been a sign in front of us, but no sign of any buildings.

We forced the doors of the car open, and the wind blasted us. I stalked towards the sign.

Dust forced its way into every crack in my clothing, each lining was an open doorway for the uninvited guest. While my body healed up quickly, the sand saturated and tore the fresh flesh, almost as fast as my body managed to fix it. Like going to the beach and getting sand in your shorts, but the sand was in hurricane like winds. Very intrusive and horribly uncomfortable.

"NOW WHAT?" Terra shouted over the din.

"NO IDEA!" I raised my arms up in an emphatic shrug.I reexamined the sign and realized that a button hid in plain sight between the words Deep Diner. It was camouflaged, a small one, but a button none the less.

Upon finding it, I pointed it out to Terra and he shrugged. He made a pushing gesture with his right pointer finger. I figured what the hell, and pressed down on the button, it gave a satisfying click when I pressed it. I waited for a bell, a response, or even an explosion.But nothing happened, so I pushed it again a few times. It clicked each time.

I turned to protest to Terra when a deafening foghorn split the air. Clear as day over the sound of the coursing winds. Terra covered his ears as a dull ache in my head crescendoed too.

A line formed in the sand and the ground rumbled. It grew wider, and sand spilled into the fresh chasm. It reminded me of how Abysm opened up to transport people downward, but this time the building physically rose from the dirt to greet us. Two large doors, opening upward and outward, appeared before us like a pair of hands opened to show you something they had caught. Sand whipped past us as it blasted from the erected doors. The aperture opened wider until we saw a set of polished metal stairs unfolded in front of us.

I turned to Terra and pointed at the car. "You stay until I come back!" I shouted at him. He gave me a thumb up and walked over to the car.

I turned and descended the stairs that had appeared, to a pair of dusty glass doors, the kind you would push to walk into a gas station from back in the days. Matte metal frames, a handlebar with a flat piece of steel you pushed to open the doors. They even had the old stickers that said Push, on them.

I lowered my goggles around my neck, they were helpful, but did leave quite a divot in my temples after a while. The migraine bouncing about in my head didn't help either. I placed my hands on the door and pushed them open. Papers from a basket kicked up and whipped forward in a frenzy. I turned and with some effort, forced the doors shut behind me.

After the wind had subsided inside, the welcome scent of

deep fried food wafted into my nostrils. My mouth watered, even though I wasn't particularly hungry.

That was how people became overweight, by not being hungry, but having to deal with their olfactory senses. It really made you want to eat anyways. This diner looked like the kind of place that had a killer chicken fried steak too. I loved the taste of food, but it seemed like my body didn't need it anymore. While I contemplated consumables, a husky broad-shouldered man with a thick bristly beard stood in an apron behind a wooden podium. He had a look of brief recognition in his face, it was fleeting, as his face swapped the look with a broad smile, almost as broad as his shoulders. He looked at me and said, "Howdy! Welcome to the Deep Diner! How many in yer party?"

I was taken aback, not by his demeanor, but the fact that he had absolutely no aura. I didn't understand it. Every person I had met up until that point in my existence had shown an aura of some kind. What made that man the exception?

I answered him.

"Umm, we have three." I help up three fingers, my pinky, ring finger, and middle finger.

"Any children?" he asked as he chuckled.

"No, just adults," I said. I would have considered a joke about Maddy, but this wasn't the time. I watched as he grabbed three laminated menus from a wooden slot adorned on the wall. He then grabbed three tightly rolled linens with silverware in them, and motioned me over. I raised a hand up to halt him momentarily.

"Forgive me, dinner in a minute. I have a car parked outside with an injured woman in the backseat." He chuckled gaily.

"I'm very aware of yer predicament my amigo! We got yer buds being tended to already. So, don't worry your head none, and come have a seat. The other guy should be in soon." As he said this, the door opened and Terra walked inside, beating his jacket with snapping slapping motions.

The man with the menus shot a scolding look towards Terra.

"Mind the carpet bucko." The large man told Terra as he pointed to the cadre of dust falling onto the spotless floor. Terra looked around at the trail of dust he had dumped everywhere. "Sorry," he said and offered a sheepish smile.

The man raised an eyebrow and sighed.

"Ain't no problem here! Just tryna keep it upta code," he said in his southern accent. It sounded forced, but it had been a long time since I had spoken to someone from the south. I wasn't an expert on it either. It was possible everything about this man could be a front. The no aura thing really threw me off.

"Hey, if you knew that we had someone in the car up top and my friend here, why did you ask me how many we had?" I asked the bear of a man.

He chortled a bit. "Ain't you never heard of courtesy before? I got cameras on every bit of this place. I know what's going on at all times in my place of business, but I prefer to keep things cordial if that's alright with you my young friend?"

"That's fair enough," I said accepting his answer, it was very difficult to get a read on someone when they don't have an aura.

"If'n you'll follow me please." He turned and walked through a curtain.

The entrance featured a bevy of different things. A coat rack, old photos, and a counter with an old register behind it. Dated pictures of rolling plains covered the wall, Johnny Cash sang in the background. The place seemed empty as far as I could tell, aside from the guy.

My presumptions were wrong however. He led us into the dining room with a small stage in the corner. Four windows with wooden frames, were lit up by background images of a city, sparkled with reflections of the other diners enjoying their meals. Seven others by my count, including the server, Terra, myself, and Maddy, wherever she had been taken to. Plus, I guessed there'd be a cook. That made twelve overall, a good number. I had to keep an eye on those things. We sat down and he handed us each a menu.

"Well howdy ya'll, my name is Avery. This here is my motel slash restaurant, The Deep Diner! We got us eight rooms, aside from my own, and Buck's room. We got two open right now, twenty partials a night. We got Buck taking care of your lady friend in the healing room, forty partials for her, medicine is expensive you know." He grinned. "We got food, drink, and music if you so wish. We ain't got much in the way of water though, plenty of good ol' hooch though!" He guffawed and his body shook. "Them bottles range in prices, but no more than a partial er two to set you back." He smiled that gigantic grin of his again, I noticed he had a chipped front tooth. The man seemed so familiar to me, but I couldn't figure out why.

"I ain't too worried if you ain't got the partials right now, I'm always willing to take compensation in some form or another!" He snickered again at this.

I looked at Terra and he looked at me. Both of us were a bit at odds at what to say.

"Can I see my friend?" I asked Avery cautiously, not sure of Maddy's status or particular whereabouts.

"Mmhmm, right after you sign this waiver saying you're good for partials or trade." He smiled, his brown eyes were heavy lidded and popped out a bit from his face.

"Paperwork..." he rolled his eyes. "The worst, right?" He handed me a clipboard with a pen tied to it with a small piece of string. I looked down and the paper had lots of lines to read. You've got to be fucking kidding me. I didn't have the time, nor did I care an iota about the idea of paperwork. He then pointed to the line that said signature, I scratched my name on it. I expected him to hand it to Terra, but then I remembered he looked four-teen still, and he probably thought I was responsible for him.

The idea of paperwork in this world seemed ridiculous, like

he'd come find me and kill me if I didn't pay him back the pittance I owed him? I guess he needed a way of finding balance, some form of normality. I imagined he probably still kept up on his taxes.

He looked over the paperwork and nodded in satisfaction. He then put the paperwork on the table.

"Well, here she is." He reached up and pulled an extendable mechanical arm attached to a monitor from the ceiling. He flipped through the channels until I could see Maddy lying supine on a gurney with bandages on her shoulder and head. A hunched, misshapen man pressed an ice pack, or some kind of pack of sorts, against her head.

The man looked back towards the camera and put down the pack. "What's the damage Buck?" Avery asked as he placed his ham sized hand on his hip.

The hunched over man grabbed a white board sitting on the table, rubbed it down with a filthy rag, and began to scribble on it.

I glanced over at Terra, and he bit his lip in confusion as he watched.

The hunched man lifted it to the screen and it read "All is well, by evening more'n'likely." Hell, his handwriting even had an accent. Avery then shoved the monitor back up and spread his arms out in front of him.

"Well then! She will be ok by this evening if Buck says so! He's the best fix it man I've ever had." He slapped Terra on the shoulder. Terra rocked forward from the impact. "A real whiz with surgeries, not to mention a mean cook! He could make a hog leap into an oven, just to be cooked by him!"

"Umm, it's always light outside though." Terra rubbed his shoulder and addressed the fact that Maddy would be ok by evening.

"There isn't really an evening anymore," I said in agreement.

"Not in here! It'd be damn near impossible to keep this heap running if there weren't no night no more." Avery exclaimed. "It's night time in a few hours, mind you. You'll see." He patted his hand on my shoulder and then walked off.

Too familiar. I wanted to say I knew him. I just couldn't place why, where, or how.

"You ok?" Asked Terra after studying the look on my face as I watched Avery walk away.

"Yeah, just a fleeting thought," I said and kept my wonderance to myself.

After that, I ordered a beer and waited around until I could get Maddy back in shape, no reason to go after someone based on a gut feeling.

Terra ordered some garlic fries, they looked like they came from the freezer section at Smith's. I seemed to remember the shape, they looked like little waffles with minced garlic on top. I didn't imagine they'd be making their own fries down here.

We sat for what seemed like an eternity. Not much conversation passed between us, we both sat patiently and waited. I did check the menu for a chicken fried steak, but my appetite had dwindled to nothing.

I wasn't sure if the fact that I said I'd kill him if Maddy died, kept him quiet, or if he was just genuinely tired. He said she'd be ok, and him being one of those Virtues, I trusted him, somewhat. His aura was my guiding light.

I couldn't shake the feeling of Avery's hand on my shoulder though, and the fact he didn't have an aura was beyond weird.

I watched the other patrons of the establishment, they sat quietly as well, casting glances our way on occasion. Everyone wore cliché' country clothing. Plaid shirts, cowboy hats, tight pants, and boots although no one was in spurs, I considered that they wouldn't have too many horses around here anymore. Seemed that most people there, the men anyhow, liked to grow their facial hair out. Bushy beards, sideburns that stuck out, and exaggerated moustaches curled at the ends with bits of wax.

I ran my hand over that beard of mine and imagined I must have fit in somewhat.

The thing that did stand out to me was that they were all spotless. Not a bit of sand on them. Probably Avery's doing. Since he chided Terra and I for the sand when we entered. Guess he just liked to have a clean restaurant. Possibly a pet peeve of his.

The patrons were fair skinned though too, which struck me as odd because everyone else I'd come across was very weather beaten, leathery skinned, and well-tanned. I guessed these people may have lived there, and had adapted to a lifestyle from it? Again, just guesswork.

Avery came to the table to check on us regularly. I watched him closely every time, but he never placed his hand on me again. I felt at odds about this, on one hand he could have known my past, on the other he could just be someone trying to make it out there in that deserted space.

I polished off around six bottles of amber beer before my stomach rejected the thought of an ounce more. It didn't take my mind off of my concerns like I'd hoped for, it niggled at me still.

I felt compelled to drink, making me wonder if I had battles with alcoholism in the past, perhaps an addictive personality that led me to pass out and wake up on a gurney one night? Who knows? My life was a whole hell of a lot more interesting than before at least.

Deep in my thoughts, I turned my attention to the bar when Avery announced the evening had arrived. I looked at a fluorescent sign for Hodge Podge Brew that had a clock in it, stuck at 1:43. The same time on the clock at the restaurant Maddy found me at, my head swam. I blinked away the haze and rubbed my eyes.

The lights in the room dimmed, and the music changed to some slower country music. The cityscape in the windows shifted.

The backdrop went dark with makeshift twinkling lights, imitating night time. That must be what Avery spoke about before.

The other people in the bar moved around, some began slow dancing with others, some drank booze, and one dark haired girl sat on her own in the corner. She leaned back against the wall and propped her boots onto the chair across from her. She had a long neck bottle pouring amber liquid into her mouth.

She tilted her hat back and stared at me with gorgeous dark brown eyes. I met her stare with curiosity, she looked down at her hip. She had a long-barreled pistol sitting there, when I looked back up, she nodded upwards behind me.

I really needed to start paying more attention to things behind me.

I turned to see Avery standing over me, he stroked his beard from cheek to chin. His large form leaning over the table. "You gents done?" he offered. "Time to clean up for me. Figur'd you fellas may want to get some shuteye." He smiled and placed a key down on the table, grinning at me.

"Your lady friend won't be comin' round til' the morning though. Ol' Buck says she's sleeping it off. She's got some metabiotics in her now, they're working to mend the wounds. Takes time, but it'll do her right." His large teeth set together in a broad grin.

Terra looked at me. "I guess we could try to get some rest, I'm running low on fumes. Just sitting on my butt without people trying to kill me has been great so far, but exhausting. If I actually do manage to get some sleep, I'll be good to go in the morning."

I nodded, and looked back over to the corner where the brown eyed girl sat. Just an empty table there now. Her bottle perched high and dry on her table. A crumpled-up napkin and some partials rested on the table in her absence.

"Can I see Maddy again?" I asked Avery as Terra got up from the table to head to the room.

"Well sure," he said cordially.

He grabbed the monitor from the ceiling and pulled it down for me to see. Maddy laid supine still, covered in a blanket, she breathed evenly, and slept hard. I thought if I could hear her, she'd be snoring loudly. I felt like she'd be ok, so I nodded at Avery and got up from the table and followed Terra out.

I scratched my beard and thought about the Avery situation. It was possible I might've been overthinking it. That we had never met, or if we did, it could have been a chance thing. What could he possibly know about me anyways? Avery looked back at me and stopped. Terra stopped and looked back at him.

"What's troubling you? Got something on yer mind? Don't mean to pry, but you got trouble written all over yer brow." He looked me dead in the eyes with his large coffee colored eyes.

"Nothing. I just wonder if we haven't met before?" I asked him straight out.

He didn't blink. He looked me dead on and shook his head. "If we'd have met son, it'd have been many years ago. I don't get out much anymore like I used to. I apologize if I can't recollect you though, I've met so many people. None that stuck around long anyhow." He smiled innocently.

"If I remember anything though, I'll be sure to come find you." He grinned.

I imagined he was telling the truth about that at least.

We continued down the hallway.

I stayed back from Avery as he walked in front of us. He even smelled familiar, he wore a cologne that I knew. I still didn't trust him; I just didn't know how to address it without knowing for sure. I would really kill for an aura about now. The room was small and cramped, it couldn't have been any larger than ten by ten. Two bunks lined the walls when you walked right in the room. One on either side of the room, fresh sheets, and a poster on the wall that said Howdy in bright gold foil letters with an exclamation point.

Avery must've picked up what I felt. "Now, I reckon it's small, but it's mighty accommodating. Just wait til' you plop on down on that mattress, finest you'll find anywhere!" He grinned as he patted the comforter on the bed.

"You two go on and hunker down, feel free to knock off any leftover dust from outside in the corners, we've got a small vacuum that'll suck it right out of here!" He pointed at the small opening on the floor near the corners.

"Set that alarm clock over there for..." He looked at his wrist watch. "Set it for 11:11," he smiled brightly. "Guess you'd better make a wish! Could be a good omen!"

I wished I could actually get some sleep, I wasn't sure I remembered what true respite felt like. Avery turned and walked back to the door. "You boys have a good night. We'll keep the wolves away." He shut the door and the room went dark. The light from the window being the only light we had.

Terra yawned and rubbed his eyes, he looked like he could've passed out at any minute, I guessed the day had worn on him more than he let on. I never liked the idea of sleeping in an underground bunker, too confined. I felt ok about Maddy, but something about the place and the patrons didn't sit well with me. The way they stared at us, how clean they were, and how pale they looked. Didn't seem like it fit in with the rest of this world.

Avery's big hand on my shoulder gnawed in my mind still. I couldn't explain it. Then again, I'd just met a kid who was supposed to be in his thirties, but looked fourteen, and could control the earth with his mind. So really, what the hell do I know? I stretched my arms upwards and arched my back.

I lied down on the bed expecting a soft cushion, but what I got was a thud. It wasn't even remotely comfortable. I couldn't complain though. I mean, in comparison to a gurney, that bed could've been a cloud.

But it made my body ache when I lied down. I rolled onto my

back and stared at the ceiling, hoping to let my thoughts cause the aches to subside. Terra turned on his bed.

"Khadim, did you see the way those people looked at the restaurant?" Terra said from the other side of the miniscule room.

"Yep." I nodded. "Figured they were part of the charming culture here."

"I guess so, but they didn't seem too hospitable, I always read that country places like this were supposed to be filled with people who were super nice. All I got today were stares, aside from Avery anyhow," he said.

"I don't know Terra; the world isn't what it used to be." I shifted my pillow under my head. "Not sure how you've dealt with it for so long."

He sighed. "Honestly, I kind of got drafted into this whole Virtue ordeal, Solace found me."

"Solace found you?" My curiosity piqued.

"Yep, she's my hero. I had no way to fend for myself out there alone. I passed out on the side of the road after I had walked for hours trying to find my way. You've seen it in all its grandeur, it's a wasteland. I would have died from that sun if she hadn't shown up when she did." He told me.

"Lucky you, why were you alone?" I turned to look at him. He stared down at the floor for a moment, and then looked back up at me. His hazel eyes were full of pain and he wiped tears from his cheeks.

"My folks and I were out there just trying to survive. We were doing a fairly decent job of it too until a group of bikers came and wrecked everything I ever cared about." He paused for a moment and took a deep breath, his chest rising and falling heavily.

He spoke in a whisper.

"I remember watching them smash my father in the head with a hammer, each blow caving his skull in deeper." He looked up and fixed me with a cold stare. "Khadim, they laughed as his head collapsed. My father kept his brown eyes on me the whole time. Those eyes that had comforted me for as far back as I could remember." He shook his head. "He kept telling me it'd be ok."

"When they broke his skull open, I watched my father's life leave his body. They'd knocked my Mother unconscious and tied her to one of the bigger bikes. The men told me what they were going to do to her. That they would have their way with her, and then throw her to the dogs for scraps." The light reflected off his tear strew face.

"I sat there, and I didn't do anything." He wiped his face. "I watched as they took my mother and drove away with her, I sat next to my dead father and cried." He leaned back on the pillow for a minute.

"After that, I walked off into the wastes to die. My life meant nothing after that moment."

Damn. I thought to myself

"Did you ever find your mother?" I asked.

"No," he said. "I was so worthless then, I should have fought those bikers, and tried to save my parents."

This is why he had the sadness in his aura. Guilt. I contemplated.

"They would've killed you too," I said as I looked down at the floor, not wanting to see his reaction.

"I know, I was so pathetic they just left me to die on my own," he said quietly. "I wasn't a threat to them."

"I sat there for what could've been days. I don't know…"

"And then there she was, in all her glory, Solace." he said while smiling brightly.

"She found me curled up on the side of the road, as good as dead. I don't know how I survived up until that point to be honest. I thought I'd die on that road, and didn't care if I did or not, but my body kept fighting back for me. I felt dehydrated and delusional, but my body remained strong. I thought it could've been adrenaline, but it turned out I had bigger things on the horizon.

Solace rescued me, she showed me how to be who I am today." He coughed out a laugh as he wiped his eyes.

"Over the years, I accepted who I came to be, things just sort of fell into place for me. I've worked hard ever since then to become a better person, not to be weak, and to do what's right no matter the circumstances."

"It's good you found your own path." I said to him as I started to drift off.

"Thanks Khadim, I hope she can do the same for you." I still doubted that she would have all the answers I needed, but it didn't hurt that she saved a kid in need.

Terra's breathing slowed as he crested into sleep.

I turned my attention to the ceiling.

I don't know when it happened, but the world fell away as I melted through the bed and drifted into a world of darkness.

CHAPTER 10
THE DREAM SEQUENCE

CLAWS MET SWORDS, cloven hooves trampled tattered wings, Bright. White beams of light pierced through hearts of the darkest black. The pandemonium strewn battlefield pulsed alive as a torrent of chaos. Cheers of valor and cries of woe clashed in a cacophony that assaulted my weakened soul and rattled me to my very core.

A large milk colored demon, with a huge bulbous gut covered in pustules, roared. The school bus sized demon towered high above the field. He snatched an angel in full battle armor from the air. The figure flailed in his hands and tried desperately to impale the large demon with his golden spear, but he could not get past the demon's grip. The demon plucked the wings from the angel and bit its wounded head from his shoulders, slavering all over the rest of his body with saliva and mucus. Thick blood oozed down the body of the hulking demon.

Angels rallied to the side of their fallen comrade, an angel dressed in golden battle armor appeared amidst their ranks. He hurled a flaming spear at the demon as it turned to him. The air flashed white around the angel and the spear tore a hole through the chest of the monster and set it aflame. Fire crackled as it burned in white light. As it fell, the body melted into a pool of sickly green bile. From the remains, more demons poured forth, climbing through the new maw opened on the ground. Misshapen bodies shambled as they made their way to the angels.

A slender man dressed in black appeared on the field in the distance. Unlike the rest of the angels and demons, he stood regaled in a tight form fitting suit. His equine face shone long and pale. He wore a bowler cap that sloped down to cover his eyes. I watched him shift his gaze back and forth across the scene as he marched closer to the battle scene.

The rest of the demons charged. Angels fell one by one. Only the magnificent angel holding the flaming spear, had an answer for each new demon that arose from the last. He wielded his burning spear, melting each demon in a flurry of flames. Still, his effort remained futile as the rest of his comrades fell one by one. The demons still poured forth en masse.

Soon, the spear-wielding angel stood alone, the last surviving angel pitted against the fields of demons.

A flurry of blows from the angel had decided the fate of the remaining demons. They swarmed him, but to no avail. He remained far too strong for them. Bursts of white light flashed out over the corpses of his fallen friends. Smoking pools of bile littered the battlefield. For now, the demons had been vanquished.

With the battle at an end, the angel fell to his knees and wept.

The sound of clapping broke the new-found silence. The man in black mockingly applauded as he strolled over to where the angel stood.

Upon seeing the approach of the man in black, the angel looked up at him through the eyes of his helmet.

"Maurelius. Stay where you are, I have no desire to hear your chiding this day." The angel stood to face him.

The man in black stopped and held his palms out in a gesture of innocence.

"Goethe. Are you not sated now?" He asked with a hint of a grin. "You have slaughtered the dark this day! What glories you shall have!" He spread his arms out and then clapped enthusiastically while grinning from ear to ear.

Goethe, the angel, pulled a dagger from his hip and sliced deep wounds into his arms. Old scars lined his arms. Each time the wind caused his regalia to shift, I could see more scars across his body.

Crimson blood seeped through his fresh wounds and caked his arms. Goethe's white flowing cloth flapped energetically in the wind, drenching itself in his blood. He removed his golden helmet to reveal a horribly scarred face.Goethe put down the blade and turned his gaze to the man in black.

"What is happiness? I fight endlessly to protect our realm from demons. To serve what purpose? To protect a realm of men who grow fat and sate their needs by supping upon lust and pleasantries?

The women tend to these men and they are tossed out after they are used. Men are not worth protecting. These angels who died today will be honored by him," the angel pointed skyward. "to be revived to protect these fools again? Humans are arrogant and each one a fool larger than the last."

The man in black took his cap off and revealed a tightly cropped head of platinum blonde hair. He pulled a cloth from his pocket and wiped his brow, staring into the eyes of Goethe. "You chose this path. You said *you* wanted power, power to make humanity better." He put his hat on again. "Tut-tut." He wagged his finger. "Typical human, figuring he knew what could make the world better. What could you possibly know better than God?" He shook his head as he looked skyward.

Maurelius exhaled loudly.

"You have overstayed your welcome here. We believe we'd be better off with someone..." he paused, "with a more malleable mindset."

Maurelius lifted his plowshare from the ground and placed the point directly in the sternum of Goethe. The scarred angel grabbed at the wound as crimson blood poured down his chest and spattered the cold glistening metal of Maurelius's weapon. Goethe looked up at the black figure as his fluids saturated the ground in a sea of red. "There will be another who sees through the game. One who will guide the world back to its balance. Equilibrium will co—" He choked on his final words as Maurelius shoved the plowshare in deeper, crushing the life from Goethe.

"I'll end you, and all of those who come after you who don't follow our rules. This is our world, not God's."

The man in black then turned and looked me directly in the eyes.

"I see you." He screamed a piercing howl and charged like a demon at me.

My eyes opened as I yelled out.

My body dripped with sweat, soaking my thin white hotel sheets. I turned and sat up, pressing my hands through my hair. My head was soaked and my hair matted against my skull. I wiped my clammy hands on my shorts.

Shit, they were filthy. I realized I hadn't changed since I stole Reese's clothing. What I wouldn't give for a shower. I grabbed my clothes from their heap on the floor and shook them out on the floor near the vacuum.

I hit a button and the engine in the wall whirred into life, it siphoned every grain of dirt and sand from the ground. I banged the boots together and a cascade of dust and dirt followed, quickly sucked into the wall as well. I grabbed the sheet from the bed and wiped down my body to clear up the sweat, seeing as they didn't have towels or a shower, this would have to be the next best thing available.

Getting myself thoroughly cleaned with the available resources felt good. The sand had been rubbing against my skin and making

me itch. Good thing I could heal, or it wouldn't be nearly as pleas-
ant. I imagined Terra didn't have a lot of problem with it, seeing as
he could control the earth. I bet that meant he could control sand
too. Good thing I had him down here with me. I looked over at
the night stand where the clock resided and it read 1:43, this joke
was getting old. I moved the hand ahead a minute or two. It made
me feel more at ease.

I slid the pants over my legs and buttoned up, my legs being
free of sand was a welcome relief. I pulled my shirt over my head
and onto my torso. I look around for my jacket, it laid next to the
bed in a pile. I leaned down to pick up my jacket from the ground
and heard a loud clang from underneath it.

Terra stirred a moment, when he didn't wake up, I looked
back to see what had made the noise. I didn't remember putting
anything in my pockets that would've fallen out.

I slowly lifted my jacket up and found a dagger lying there
on the ground. I grabbed the handle and picked it up and turned
it around in my hands. Fresh blood coated the blade, I wiped it
off on the sheets. I knew this knife, it was the very same one that
Goethe used in my dream to cut himself. What the hell did that
mean? How did it get there?

The door exploded open behind me. Instincts kicked in and
I rolled back towards the window. Terra shot up in his bed looking dazed. The cowgirl from the bar sucked in a deep breath and
looked at us both, the handle of the door in her left hand and a
smoking pistol in the other. "Let's go! These idiots are coming after
you Constant!" I pocketed the dagger and lifted my goggles to my
eyes, it said *Rachel Power*. She had the same title as Maddy, odd.

I looked around the room and got my jacket on, I had everything with me. Ok, good, with the goggles on, I looked up at the
window. Wouldn't you know it, of course the damned thing was a
two-way mirror. I could see a camera monitoring the room on the

other side of it. These goggles were a double-edged sword. If I wore them, Jolt saw everything. If I didn't, I felt like missed the obvious.

"Jolt?" I asked.

"You'd better go K-man," he answered. "Seems you've ended up in a real life snake pit!"

"Do I want to know?" I asked.

"Not really man, you went silent for a while. If the goggles aren't on, I can't interface with your neurological sensors."

Good to know.

"If Maddy were awake, she would've told you to hit the skids too man, that kid is sharp!" he told me.

Maddy. Fuck.

"Rachel, how do we get my friend out?" I asked.

"She's already kicked the tires, she's bolting as we speak." Rachel said as she spun around to look down the hallway.

Terra threw his things together and stood ready to roll, he looked at Rachel and nodded. We all headed in to the hallway. A dead man laid on his face on the floor by our doorway, he had two smoking holes in his chest. Didn't have to be a genius to figure out what'd happened here. We crossed through the hallway and into the dining room where Avery and five others stood.

I took a mental count. Avery, plus five strangers. Buck was probably dead if Maddy got out, the guy in the hall, me, Maddy, Rachel, and Terra. All twelve accounted for, good. I turned my attention to the scene at hand. When I looked up and saw Avery, it all made sense. The goggles had come through when my auras had failed.

Avery Fallen Virtue Life

"Shit."

Avery opened his arms up in a halting motion.

"Whoa there!" he spouted. "What's with the fireworks Megan?"

I realized he had addressed Rachel.

Two reports sounded loudly in succession.

She shot him in the chest twice, didn't hesitate for a second. The acrid scent of gun powder filled the air, and like that my chances at asking him about my past had probably vanished.

The other five spread out across the room. Rachel extended her right arm out and shot one more before she could get too far. The young woman took the shot through the throat, she reached up to stop it, but we all know how that goes. We were down to four.

Two of the women leapt behind the bar, and one onto the stage, they were trying to get an angle on us. Rachel holstered her pistol and looked at me. "This is your show Constant; I'm just trying to get you to Solace."

The lone man shuffled in front of us hunched over on all fours. His bones began to shift within his body. They snapped and popped in protest. His arms and legs transformed. Bones forced their way through the skin. His face shifted into canine features, looking more lupine. The other three around the room were all doing the same thing. Their bodies shifted and changed, "Werewolves?!" I muttered to myself. "You've got to be fucking kidding me."

Terra looked frustrated, about faced, and headed to the front doors.

"Screw this." "Use your earth stuff!" I shouted at him.

"There is literally no dirt in here! I already tried! It's spotless! The outside is sealed in metal and I can't get through it!"

Great. Meet a guy who can manipulate the earth, and end up in a fight where there is no fucking earth to manipulate. Jesus.

I'd left the maul and pistol in the car, and only had what lay around to fight with. I grabbed a chair and broke the leg off with my foot. Picking up the pointed club, I held it out. The thing in front of me looked like a bald wolf, or maybe one of those cats that had no hair.

"Coyote." Jolt said in my head. "They're coyotes, like werewolves, but coyote versions. Ugly bastards."

"Listen Constant, I've never met Avery, but I can tell you this for sure. He's probably not dead, you'd better cut through his compadres right quick my man." Jolt highlighted them on the screen.

Avery was still alive? That calmed my nerves a bit.

I leapt forward and drove the chair leg into the shoulder of the Coyote in front of me. He slapped me away. I rolled on the ground and he leapt up in the air towards my face. The other three crept into the background, I could hear them. Rachel must have been fighting one or two, she looked like she could take care of herself.

The coyote I fought landed on my chest, the wind swiftly escaped my lungs. I placed my arms on his furry collarbone and squeezed as hard as I could. Must've been a good grab, I felt a snap as his bone collapsed under the pressure. As he fell back in retreat, I spotted a smoking mark on his neck. Before I had a chance to pursue him, another leapt at my back and clawed viciously at my jacket. I heard the leather tear open. Turning around, I swung my left fist backwards, catching the damned thing in the jaw. I pivoted and charged after the new target. I dove at him, her? I didn't know anymore.

I caught it by the nape and thundered a driving blow into the thing's throat. My fist glided through the skin and into the wet parts. Steam shot from the wound as warm blood jetted down my arm and onto my jacket.

I didn't wait to see why, I pressed on until there were only unrecognizable parts above the shoulders. The soggy mist steamed and the stench of its blood nauseated me, equal parts sulfur and garbage. I turned to find the other three, and found Rachel curled up on the floor bleeding and possibly unconscious. The other two coyotes turned back and saw what remained of their friend. I turned to find Terra, I hope he didn't run away.

As if on cue, the earth shook. Tables danced back and forth, the bottles in the bar fell from the shelves, and monitors fell from the ceiling, they shook violently with the vibrations. I could see on one of the screens a dead man on a gurney with a knife sticking out of his throat. Maddy had indeed killed Buck, I turned to see Terra walk in with his arms covered in sand. I dove out of the way.

"Glass doors were a mistake." He said as the sand shot forward and pinned the two Coyotes to the wall in front of him. They kicked and scratched at the pillars of earth that held them tight.

I glanced towards Rachel again, "She's up" chimed in Jolt. As he said this, Rachel stood up and blasted the two coyotes in the face with her pistol. Both shots seemed to come from a single report. Their skulls exploded out the back of their heads, the landscape on the wall replaced with Jackson Pollock-like blood spatters. They fell to the floor dead. A single coyote remained, the one I injured earlier. He looked at us and changed back into a human. The snapping bones and grinding noises gave me a wave of nausea. He cowered next to the bar crying as he begged for his life.

"Please, wait, I didn't want this!" He yowled.

Rachel turned to me, so did Terra. I looked at the coyote and his aura showed through as purple and black. Terrified, and he wouldn't attack.

However, he had killed too many to have an aura that black. Indiscernible from the other sins because the overlay of thick jet black. I nodded at Rachel and Terra, and turned back to walk over to Avery. I didn't look to watch the Coyote's demise. I heard it.

CHAPTER 11
CAGING THE COYOTE

AVERY BREATHED DEEPLY but was clearly out cold. The shots seemed to be healing in his chest, both slugs had fallen on the floor. Looked like I would have a chance to talk to him again in the future after all. While I considered the situation, Rachel stepped heavily towards me while reloading her pistol.

Click

Click

Click

Click

I tensed at the recurring sound.

"Can you please not do that?" I asked her abruptly.

"What?" she said after flipping her cylinder back in. "The reload?"

I nodded.

"The noise?" she asked. I nodded again.

"Sorry." she said as she walked past me. "Thank you." I said to her.

I looked at Avery, his two bullet wounds were being mended slowly in front of me.

Why is healing? Is he like me?

I stared at the wounds for a minute trying to understand. I

knew Terra healed quickly, but Avery healed at about the same rate I did. We probably didn't have a lot of time.

"No, it's not the transition from beast to human. It's the metabiotics in his system mending him." Jolt told me after he read my thoughts. "They're artificial Werecoyotes, if that makes sense."

"They said that they put metabiotics in Maddy, is that the same thing? Is she going to become one of these things?" I asked out loud with a sense of fear.

Rachel heard me and shook her head.

"He uses different Metas on himself. They're more elaborate, a cocktail of sorts, and faster acting than the ones your friend got. He had other ideas for her it seemed."

"Where is she by the way?" I asked.

"Upstairs" Terra nodded towards the front. "She's the reason that the building shifted out of the ground."

I reached into my pocket and removed the dagger I found. I looked over at Avery, some of these guys were better off dead, these Virtues. I raised the dagger over his chest, but thought that I would never get to ask him about my past if I killed him now. I was a thought away from stopping already, but Jolt interjected.

"WAIT!" Jolt shouted out through the goggles. "Leave him, he doesn't know what he's doing, too much is happening too fast. Get to Solace. Lock him down here with something to think about man, I'll show you how."

Somehow, he didn't register my thoughts about Avery and my past, which seemed odd because he had picked up on everything else up so far.

I considered his words though, I didn't get why he protected these people. He kept pushing me to get to Solace. If she didn't have all these answers he kept promising, I'd come after him too. I would find my balance one way or another.

I slid the dagger carefully back into my pocket.

Maddy galloped down the stairs and ran into the restaurant.

"You're really helpless without me, huh? Look at this fucking place? A hick bar and you decided that THIS was a good place to stop for me?" She shook her head.

"This is obviously a fucking meat mill. Underground place that can seal the desert out? Might as well have named 'COME GET EATEN!' or something like that." She chuckled.

She looked at me and grinned. "Glad you're ok dude. You might be thick, but you're the most interesting person I've ever met." She looked from Rachel to Terra. "Man, Patty is going to beat your face in for her car. Who's the cowgirl?" She turned to me and thumbed towards Rachel.

Rachel answered for herself.

"I'm Rachel, I don't normally wear this stuff, but I had to fit in with these yokels to get you guys out. Solace sent me after Terra went missing." She said. "I guessed that you might end up here."

I watched Rachel explain her story and saw she was well built and muscular. She was taller than Maddy by a few inches. Strange how these people made their way into my life.

I then looked at everyone, and then at the bar. "While I appreciate that you guys are following formalities, I'd like to get out of here," I said thinking about the healing Virtue lying on the ground before me. "I want to get to Solace so I can sort this shit out."

Hopefully.

Maddy looked around the bar. "We should probably get whatever water they have, we're down to one bottle in the car." A guilty look came across her face. "I helped myself when I got out," She giggled nervously.

"You understand."

"Fine, you look for water. Terra, help me move this big bastard somewhere safe." Terra nodded and helped me find a room for him. He had the keys to the rooms in his pocket and we saw that the doors locked from the outside in, it would take him a bit to get out hopefully.

Terra's eyes closed as he concentrated on moving outside sand to where we were. The sand in the bar began to roll in unison across the floors and down the hallway.

The walls in the room seemed secure, just thick concrete walls and no beds. The front doors were open, and more sand crept its way inside in a thin line, then into a thick stream that poured into the room past Terra. It came in droves, the room filled top to bottom and sealed the large prone man to the ground. We shut the door as the sand continued to slip in through the cracks in the door. Terra filled the room to the ceiling. I locked the door with the key.

"He won't be able to move for days. If he's one of us though, he won't die. He'll be in pain, and hate us forever, but he'll live." Terra patted me on the shoulder and walked around the hallway's corner. He turned and filled the hallway with sand to further barricade the door. "I'd say that it'll take him at least a week to get out."

I stood and looked at the room with the unconscious virtue and promised I would find him again. I couldn't help the timing of life, things happened when they did. It wasn't our time to discuss things yet. "Good job with him, now go to the bar." Jolt said.

"Not really in a drinking mood." I joked.

"It's business," Jolt answered sternly.

I stepped to the bar as ordered and stood behind the counter. The goggles highlighted the ancient register. I went over to it and touched it. Electricity surged through my fingers, the drawer popped open with a click. I pulled eleven dollars from the drawer, and just like that, I was ridiculously wealthy again, oh the socks I could buy now.

"Jackpot!" Jolt said. "There is your grease for the palms of the greedy my friend! CHA CHING!" He grinned in his little monitor.

I stuffed the money that wasn't mine into the wallet that I'd taken from Anthony. I'd be willing to bet that he made more money being dead than when he was alive.

An arrow flashed in my goggles and guided me to a picture on the wall. I strolled over to it and looked into the eyes of an old Caucasian couple. A copy of the painting *American Gothic*, I believe. An old bespectacled man holding a pitch fork, and a woman with her hair up next to him. They stood in front of a barn. Ugly people, but then again, I would never buy something like this. I preferred Rothko, simple and beautiful.

I reached up and grabbed the sides. The painting came away from the wall to reveal a metal panel. Another cliché', a panel behind the painting. That shtick was so predictable.

"That's a win right there my friend!" Jolt exclaimed. "Pop that bad boy open, and do try to be careful with the painting, Mr. Wood wouldn't approve if you scuffed it up."

I stopped and looked at the painting again. No way this painting is the real deal, couldn't be. I placed the painting down against the wall on the other side just in case. I went back to the panel and touched it like Jolt asked me to do. Electricity ran through my fingers again. It thrummed as I palpated the various switches.

"That one!" he said. "Throw that switch when everyone is out, before you do that though, hit that one." One of the switches went flashing red to indicate the one Jolt talked about. I flipped the switch like he asked me to, nothing happened. "Ok, back to the other switch," he said.

"Everyone out, we're closing Deep Diner down for business," I shouted.

"Hang on a sec," Terra sauntered in carrying the broken sign he'd obviously taken from the front of the business and tossed it on the floor. "Can't have other people turning into those fuck ugly things." He gave me a thumb up and walked outside. Maddy hummed as she carried an armful of bottles with one in her mouth. She nodded at me as she headed outside. Rachel came over and grabbed a bottle of Jameson off the counter. She no longer wore her cowgirl outfit; she had changed into a red t-shirt and a pair of jeans.

"Glad that's over, hillbillies aren't my typical cup of tea." She pulled her mouth cover up and put her goggles on as she headed out the doors.

Once she had left, I hit the switch and rushed out as the building began to sink into the surface again. Motels, it seemed, were still shit in the future. From what I'd seen, most of the world was shit…

I took the stairs outside, I turned and admired the last descent of the Deep Diner. After it settled, I saw what the other switch had done.

CHAPTER 12

SERENDIPITY STRIKES AGAIN

THE GROUND SHOOK as I turned from the now sunken Deep Diner, I turned to see the results of Jolt's suggestion to hit those switches. Where there was once a flat landscape covered in dirt, there stood a two-story building with two garage doors on the front of it.

The structure that had emerged from the earth loomed over us. I looked over through an open doorway to see Maddy already standing inside of the building, she stared at a metal box on the wall. As I walked closer, I heard her shouting over the wind outside.

"Woo! These assholes had a stash!" She stood in the doorway to the garage. She frantically waved and motioned for me to come over.

The large gate on the front of the building opened as she shouted at me. At the bottom of the gate, I could see why she seemed so excited. They had a room full of old cars, and with four of us traveling together, , Pearl would be a little cramped. Things were finally going our way a bit.

"Wow," I said to Maddy.

"Right?" She chuckled.

As I dusted myself off and strolled into the room, I noted the various tools that lined the walls: wrenches, hammers, ratchets, sockets, screwdrivers, pliers, pry bars, and flashlights. Different jacks sat on the floor beside some compressors, and a few generators. The walls were decorated with various license plates from different states.

"Could we use these?" Maddy asked as she pointed my attention to something behind her.

I looked up to see what had she motioned to.

A car propped up on a lift overhead looked like an old Malibu, maybe from the nineties? Not much interest there. They had another car sitting on a lift on the ground still, a tan Corolla. Again, nothing of interest.

"Not really, these things wouldn't last long in that wasteland." I told her. "They barely made it back when they first came out."

The last row offered something more interesting within its confines. I felt like Edmund Dantés in The Count of Monte Cristo. We'd found a vast treasure that had been hidden away, just waiting for us to discover it. There sat an old Ford Camper Van. All white and it had been modified to the teeth. Its huge knobby tires helped lift it high up from the ground. I checked the door handle and was genuinely shocked to feel the door pop open.

"This though, this could work." I waved my hand at the Camper's open door.

"Yeah?" She sidled over in my direction. "Spacious?"

I stepped into the van, and saw plenty of room. "I think we could fit the entire Brady Bunch in here."

"What the hell is a Brady Bunch?" She looked perplexed.

"Never mind." All the panels inside the van were modern. The buttons, dials, all new. Only the windows were old school, you had to manually use them. I rolled one down, things seemed to be in working condition.

"Weird," I said.

"What?" Maddy looked at me through the open window of

the van. She bit at her thumbnail, I could hear her teeth click as she bit through.

"Why would everything be new, but the windows are manual?" I asked not expecting an answer.

"Electric windows are shit man; the motors break all the time. It's just way easier to use the handle, it's more rugged." She shrugged at me and spit her nail out.

"Makes sense." Her knowledge of cars could be useful at times. I flipped down the visor in the front seat, half expecting keys to fall into my hand. No such luck.

"Well?" Maddy asked.

"I'm thinking." My feet echoed off the concrete as

I jumped out of the car and walked around the back to see there was no gas panel, it seemed this van might be solar, like Pearl. That worried me because if we were going into the dark, this thing wouldn't work the way we needed it to.

I slid on my back under the vehicle, the cool floor felt good. No fuel tank, just an empty spot where it went.

Maddy plopped down on the floor to see what I saw. After seeing the missing tank, she gave her two cents. "We're going to need gas out there."

No shit.

Upon further inspection, I saw the rest of the van's underside had skid plates all over it.

"There's lots of different skid plates to protect the underside of the vehicle. Looks like there were bolts here to add one over the fuel tank. I thought there wasn't a pump to refuel, but, by using the power of deduction, there's got to be one around here somewhere." I told Maddy.

She hopped up from the ground and walked off without a word.

I slid out from under the van and scanned the room.

"Khadim, keys." Maddy said from across the room. She stood

next to a metal case on the wall that looked like she had pried open with a crowbar. The fact that she pried it open before we could try these keys didn't surprise me in the least.

"Look for one that will fit in this van." I told her.

"There are like, fifty keys in here!" She scowled and shouted snapping her hands towards the box.

"Should have a wide base, maybe say Ford, or be blue." I think I owned one of these vans in the past possibly.

"Ok," she said while turning around shrugging her shoulders. She turned back around to me. "Hey, Khadim?"

"Yeah?" I looked at her.

"You might check that door at the back of the room. I haven't looked there yet."

I turned and walked to the back room, sure enough there stood a metal door. I went with the obvious and tried the handle. It didn't budge.

I reached into my pocket and produced the keys I took from Avery. I tried key after key, but it seemed my luck had run out. Putting them back in my pocket, I considered other methods.

"Any door keys in the case?" I shouted at Maddy.

"No idea," she said. "You could come grab a bunch and try them all?"

That could take a while.

I pulled at my beard. The massive door seemed thick. I wasn't sure I could muscle my way through, but I'd give it a go.

I rammed my shoulder into the door, it didn't budge. I tried kicking the door open, it held solid. I walked over to where Maddy stood and grabbed the crowbar.

"That's what we call a skeleton key." Maddy laughed as she saw the frustration on my face.

"Let's hope so," I said and stomped back to the stuck door.

I tried prying the door open, but I couldn't find a place to angle it in for leverage though. I couldn't make purchase with it, so I said fuck it, and dropped the crowbar.

"Dude." Maddy snapped as she jumped from the noise, the keys in the box rattled back and forth.

I looked around, I didn't see Terra. He could pop that thing off. I remembered the fight with coyotes, when my fists burned through the lycans. When I killed Faul, I got some of his powers I bet. I mean, I did feel younger and stronger. I imagined it had to be more than a chemical release, right?

I placed my hand on the cold metal and thought about the sun. How much I hated its white light just endlessly pounding the earth. The way it caused my skin to darken, and how it made everything beautiful fade away.

"Whoa," Maddy said from across the room.

I looked at my hand as it turned a warm yellow. I turned my hand and looked at it, it reminded me of molten metal. It didn't burn or hurt at all, it just tingled, like pins and needles.

Maddy had come over and was staring wide-eyed at my hand. "Are you doing that? That's fucking weird man."

"Yeah," I said in staggered tones.

Was this really working?

I placed my hand over the handle and pressed on it. I felt the rigid surface resist only momentarily. It turned from a solid to a liquid. The metal sizzled and spattered onto the floor.

Maddy jumped back a step when the sizzling metal spattered the floor. The latch fell off and clanged against the floor. The door swung open.

I stared at my hand and then back at Maddy.

"Ok, not going to lie, kind of scary, but mostly awesome." Maddy grabbed my wrist and inspected my hand. "Does it hurt?"

"No, it just tingles," I told her.

"Hmm…" She tapped her chin. "You are such an interesting person Khadim. I however, need to find that key."

She turned and kicked the latch over to the side and made her way back to the key box.

I nodded at her and turned my attention back to the new room that had opened now.

After my hand returned to normal, I touched the melted metal where I opened the door. A sharp burning sensation of pain. "Shit!" I said, my finger throbbing where it connected with the metal. I placed my finger in my mouth and walked inside, figuring I would have to explore these new abilities another time.

My finger pulsed as I flipped on a light switch. The fluorescent lights flickered on slowly and the low hum of the bulbs gave me a headache. When I looked up at the room, a rush of nausea hit me hard.

I was pretty sure I knew where I'd met Avery.

Everything was the same, it was almost identical to the room I had been trapped in for years. My mind flashed back to the room I was in for all that time, the only thing missing at this moment was the incessant dripping. There were multiple gurneys, chains, and vicious tools everywhere. It was beyond eerie.

Freezers lined the walls, probably filled with organic materials. Each gurney sat empty, and wiped clean. Bloody symbols covered the walls. Just like the room I woke up inside of. Fatigue wracked my body as I became lost in the room. Leaning against the wall, I felt like I might pass out.

I shook the feeling from my mind. I would have to find Avery another time and dive into that conversation separately. He would answer every one of my questions, that's for damn sure.

As my senses returned, I looked over and saw the skid plate and the fuel tank leaning against the wall. I stalked over and grabbed the tank by the top. I rocked it back and forth, not a drop of gasoline in it. Not even the smell remained, it hadn't been used in ages. At least it wouldn't be heavy to move without the gas in it.

I heard footsteps come into the room from behind me.

"Anything good in there?" Maddy handed me a key. "I'm pretty sure this is the one." She clicked a button on the key and the horn honked on the van. She deftly pocketed the key.

When I looked at her, she furrowed her brow. "You get Pearl, I looked and that thing is an automatic. I'm driving it. It's four-wheel drive too," she said, her eyes wide with excitement. She looked back at my discovery.

"Is there gas in that?" she asked kicking the tank with her boot, a hollow sound echoed throughout the garage and her laces clattered off the floor. She really needed to tie her shoes.

"Not a drop," I said. "We'll have to find some along the way." I gestured to her untied shoe. "I'm surprised you didn't kill yourself in Terry's car with those loose laces."

"Was that a joke?" she asked. "Seems like you're in a good mood." She bent over and tied her laces.

If she only knew.

That room rocked my system. Ever since I'd woken up, it'd been an endless guessing game as to what the hell I was supposed to do next. I didn't set out looking to battle gangs, run from people with strange powers, kill them, meet others, and have some sort of destiny mixed in with all of it. I just wanted to get out of that basement and get back to living a normal life, provided someone could tell me what that looked like in that new world.

I had questioned if I did want out after I'd had a taste of the world waiting for me. But seeing that room, I was certain, I could never go back. I had to keep moving to find my peace. My goal had become to get to Solace and hopefully sort the sideshow out sooner than later. Terra and Rachel rushed into the garage from outside. Rachel shook the dust from her hair and batted it off her clothing with her hands as Terra walked calmly between the two cars.

"We didn't find anything else behind the building, just a brick wall, the door back there didn't lead to anything. Nothing but an empty area." Terra said and Rachel nodded to back him up.

"Seems like we have a new vehicle at least?" Rachel said, eying the van and materials on the walls. Maddy leaned on the front of the van and put on her best alpha face.

Terra raised a doubtful eyebrow and looked at me questioningly. "You're still taking Pearl right?"

"Yeah, I can drive her while you all ride in the van." I said. "The sand doesn't bother me," I lied.

"I'm driving the van!" Maddy said quickly and loudly like a kid proclaiming she would be the first one to get a slice of cake.

Terra and Rachel didn't protest, I wasn't sure they even noticed her comment.

"I'll ride with you if that's ok Khadim?" Terra scratched at his short-cropped hair. "I can keep the sand away with minimal effort."

I nodded in agreement. He was right, his cinnamon colored skin was completely free of any dirt or dust.

Terra walked over to the burned door of the back room, I watched as he touched the cooled metal. He turned to look at me, his hazel eyes searching me with curiosity. "In fact, we can probably replace those windows on Pearl if you don't mind using that new gift of yours?"

I was reluctant, but curious as well. We sauntered outside and left Rachel and Maddy to deal with the van. They started loading the back of the van with various tools and helpful things in case of emergency.

The wind outside roared violently and my clothes pressed tightly to my skin. I had to lean into the onslaught and push through it. Terra strode beside me, calm as ever. The dust never even touched him out here. I watched it move out of his way and around his small figure.

I thought about when he walked into the restaurant and Avery told him to not get dust everywhere, he had been covered at the time. Did he do it just for appearances? His jacket whipped in the wind, but dust avoided him. I guessed he could consciously keep the debris from his body, but he let it sit on him when he walked into a place he didn't know. If he came inside clean, it could tip off strangers that something wasn't right. We made our way over to Pearl. The front windshield seemed in decent condition still. It must've been reinforced, same with the back. The three side windows on each side were missing, along with the metal brackets that had rested in between them. I watched as Terra climbed inside the car and sat down, shutting the door and motioning for me to come over.

Looking inside the car, I saw that it had been partially filled with sand, the interior covered in dust. I couldn't even see Faul's maul resting on the backseat. Terra said something and changed my focus.

He shouted over the tempest.

"Heat your hands up like you did for the door, and stand with them out in front of you like this." He put his arms out to illustrate what he wanted me to do. "You'll need to make it hot enough you can see something starting to shape. I'll do the rest!" he shouted over the wind whipping into the side of my head. I couldn't concentrate in this mess.

"Sec, I'll handle that." He grinned and suddenly the breeze coasted around my body, all the sand on my shoulders and arms disappeared into the passing trails of wind. The sand that had crept into my hair filtered its way out. At the same time, sand burrowed inside of my clothing creeped out and into the passing torrents.

I nodded to him in appreciation.

Now that's a power.

I wanted to ask him how he knew I could heat my hands up, but I assumed it was all part of the ongoing "Don't tell Khadim shit saga," until we got to Solace. So, I let it pass.

Placing my hands in front of my palms-out, I tried the method

I used in the garage. I thought about this awful heat, and how by doing this, God only ruined *half* of the world. I hadn't seen much wildlife up here except for some dogs and lycanthropes. I looked at my hands, and watched as it began to work. My hands turned white hot. I waved them forward in front of me and held them steady like Terra had showed me.

"Good, now hotter!" Terra shouted, he had moved his hands in front of himself and mimicked my pose. I thought about how shitty this whole situation was. At that point in my life, I just wanted to find a nice quiet place in the shade to sit down, and to read a book. Yet, as the wind howled louder and louder, the desert kept ruining my thoughts. My hair whipped in the wind and slapped across my face. I hated that place.

My hands glowed brighter and I slowed my breathing as they went molten. I thought I heard Jolt in my goggles, but it must've been the wind. No monitor with his face popped up.

Terra began moving his hands up and down, like a painter might. He stroked his hands up and down, then he moved his hands outwardly. I felt resistance against my hands and kept up the heat.

"Open your hands wider," he shouted.

I did as he asked, my hands opened outwardly and he moved his hands around further. I caught a nasty glare from in front of me, a reflection of the sun. Using the sand from the air, he controlled the individual grains, combined with the heat from my hands, and molded glass right in between us. Incredible.I watched as he shaped the dark black glass to fit within each slot in the door, three in all. He pinched the ends of the dark black glass, shaping them, ensuring each new window pane was slim enough to fit into the empty slots. I continued along with him to each side of the vehicle and it got easier as I went. The control of the heat eased more and more. Every time I thought of the sun, and how much it bothered me, the more control I had. If this was power was controlled by means of irritation, I'd have the hang of it by the end of the week.

"How did we make the glass dark?" I asked him.

"I used your heat to burn the grains and turn them darker. I figured the shade couldn't hurt in this sun." Terra grinned.

Smart kid.

"Indeed." Jolt made his presence known.

Where have you been? I thought.

"The J-Man deals in information my fine sun powered friend. I did some research on our new pal we met. Somehow, he got off the radar a fair bit, he's off his rocker for damn sure too. Not sure how we missed him," Jolt exclaimed. "He's been logged and documented for further research in the future. He won't be around for a bit anyhow."

Terra grinned wide at me and got out of the car, pulling the sand out from inside the car. The current danced into the torrent of thrashing wind.

"Fun huh? But we should get a move on, I have a feeling our buddy is awake." He motioned to the spot where the restaurant had submerged.

"You sealed him in there though." I reminded him.

"I don't know what he's capable of. I just did what you asked me to do. He shouldn't be able to move, but I know little tremors man, it's kind of my thing. That's him, he is awake, and struggling." Terra finished with the sand in the car and slammed the door. We both turned and headed into the garage. Maddy reclined in the driver's seat smoking a cigarette, her feet hanging out of the window. Rachel looked up at us as we entered the room, standing alone covered in grease and sweat, her hands filthy with a rag sticking out of her back pocket. "We're set. No thanks to our friend here," she said pointing at Maddy as she slammed the back doors of the van shut loudly.

Maddy sat up and flicked ash out of the window onto the

garage floor. She blew a cloud of white smoke in annoyance as she sat the driver's seat forward. "What?! Look, I'm still healing up ok? Plus, I'm not into the whole manual labor thing. I'm more about the driving thing. You'll see," she said unapologetically. "You're really great at all that stuff you did."

Rachel ignored her and looked at me. She wiped her forehead with the rag and grinned. She had a really charming smile.

"We have gas somewhere?" she asked. A pink bubble burst from her lips, she sucked it back in and resumed chewing her gum. I shook my head. "We'll have to find something on the way. Grab a hose in case." I looked up at the walls, most of it empty now. Perhaps, I should have examined the room before making what I thought was a good suggestion.

"Already did, along with a ton of tools and the spare I found in here." She raised an eyebrow and grinned again. "I also loaded up most of everything here, the good stuff anyways." The mischievous look on her face shifted into daggers when she looked at Maddy.

At that, Maddy turned the ignition on inside the van. It made a loud guttural roar. "Oh yeah," she flicked her cigarette into the garage. She rolled up the window and looked at me, motioning with her hands she poked her wrist to mimic a watch. Terra and I headed toward Pearl, as Rachel climbed into the passenger seat of the van.

Terra and I picked up our pace and ran toward Pearl. The sand pelted me as I moved. I didn't want to stick around and see what Avery might be capable of when he wasn't caught off guard. I hoped he would stay locked up at least long enough for us to leave.

We followed Jolt's GPS, he could patch it through to the van as well. We communicated through the radio. Maddy complained the whole time she didn't have any music to listen to, and that we were going too slow across the dangerous terrain. We were already having to dodge cars along the way, checking periodically for full tanks of gas to siphon.

I reminded her that the last time we sped down a freeway, we ended up flipping Pearl over to avoid killing a kid in the middle of the road. It must've sunk in, because she didn't complain for a solid five minutes after that.

It didn't take long to get enough gas to fill the van's fuel tank. Luckily, Pearl was already topped off. The roadway seemed like something happened in the area to congest the streets. Perhaps a crash caused traffic, and people abandoned their vehicles in the road and ran. My mind wandered as I guessed endlessly about the past.

The drive seemed uneventful compared to the rest of our adventures over the past few days. We drove by a gang of bikers off on the side of the road, but they barely glanced in our direction. Maybe they were searching for a straggling pedestrian they could jump without incident. Not that I could imagine a hitchhiker having too much in the way of valuables. Violent people tended to be violent just for the sheer joy of it. Power over another individual. Power was a potent drug. Once you got a dose, you didn't want to part ways with it. It also deludes your thoughts and convictions, made you stray from the original plot you had in life.

I imagined Ouroboros to be full of people like that. Yggdrasil would be worse, no doubt. My faith in our journey dwindled. Though it may have been the only option I had for answers.

I could see a dip in the horizon, a black area looming in the distance. We were coming upon the dark quickly, according to the GPS, we'd be there in about half an hour. Jolt gave us the rundown of what to expect.

"There will be demons, make no mistake. If you get out of the car, there will be a fight. You'll have about an hour of barreling through enemy territory. "No one has won the war yet; the battle still lingers. The demons out there are aimless evil," he hesitated, then followed up. "I'm not sure the full amount of demons that will be out there, more than likely we should see all sorts. Word of advice? If you hit one?"

"Yeah?" I asked.

"Keep going," he said.

I grunted to let him know I understood.

"Fuck yeah," Maddy shouted. "You're telling me I get to hit things in the road? In a massive vehicle, at high speeds?" She giggled and drummed her hands on the steering wheel. "This is the life!" I heard the van's horn honk several times.

"You are going to want to hit those high beams too my man. Demons hate bright lights of any sort. The brighter, the better. You should also watch for traps in the road. The goggles should keep things pretty evident, but you can't risk driving too slow. If you give them a chance, the Leviathan demons will pluck your car right off the road. They'll break the car open and suck out the juicy bits, if you get my meaning." Jolt tightened his jaw and rubbed his collar on the monitor.

"I'm willing to bet we're going somewhat off the beaten path then?" I asked.

"Yes, no way you make it just on the freeway alone once we hit the dark," he said. "I'll need you to keep the goggles on you at all times too. So I can charge any light sources that might be around, odds are they have broken all the bulbs, but you never know what tricks ol' Jolt can come up with!" He smiled on the monitor.

More like he didn't want to miss anything that happened.

"Aside from that, you will want to look for the gates. Once you get to them, I can patch us in. They should have enough light on the outside to ward off the demons. Just head towards the lights."

I glanced in the mirror at the van, it was covered in extra headlights. I bet whoever put that thing together had driven through the dark before.

All in all, this sounded like an hour of sheer hell.

CHAPTER 14
THE PATH TO DARKNESS

As we crested into darkness, something popped into my head.

"The promises God makes in the light, does not change when the sun sets."

What a bunch of bullshit.

The darkness enveloped the car. Once my eyes adjusted, I could see the surrounding area as fires burned in the night. It must have been a suburb at some point.

Street signs stood vigil over the madness. Hollowed out homes sat empty and lifeless, covered in moving figures too dark to see. The windows all blasted out from some past transgression.

In the distance, I heard wails of agony and pain, some tortured soul who got caught on their way to Ouroboros. The air smelled of iron and blood, the sulfur smell just at the edge of my senses.

Crosses hung upside down with remaining corpses attached to them by barbed wire, and nails. Individuals who were crucified long ago, left to rot and waste away. A murmuration of tiny starling sized demons flew through the night overhead. They chittered endlessly as they snapped their jaws. The sound made my skin prickle. I watched as they flew in various patterns ahead of us.

You would see a shadow in the corner of your eye, but when you turned to see what was there, it had vanished. This happened frequently as we drove. It was the sort of thing to keep you on edge. We were being watched, but unable to see by what.

Many different horrors lurked in this area of the world. I personally didn't want to meet any of them.

We drove with the lights off to hopefully gain some distance in the dark before we were discovered. I knew it wouldn't last, but I looked to gain any advantage I could find. We barely breathed as Terra and I looked on in horror of our surroundings. We were only able to make it a mile or so into the night before we ran into trouble.

BOOM

I ran head on into something small in the roadway, feeling thankful for the snowplow on the front of the car. Pearl began to buck up and down in the road violently, and I looked around but couldn't see what caused it, so I hit the high beams.

A chorus of maddening shrieks erupted from all around us.

The smell of urine and musk poured through the interior vents. My eyes watered from the smell. I peered out of my window and saw something that turned my stomach.

A sea of cat-sized demons covered our entire path. As if all the stray cats of an entire city had been turned into these...things. Their waxy surfaces presented a dull glow running throughout them. When the lights from Pearl hit their milky bodies, they retreated to the darkness. Maddy kicked the lights from the van on and they ruptured into flames, you could hear the sickening pops as we drove over and through them.

These demons hissed at us with bioluminescent eyes, that reflected the light. Their skin stretched tightly over their bones. They were horrible to look at.

The lights poured forth and covered every side of us for a thousand feet easy. Every one of the demons clawed and ran as fast as they could, the less agile burst and fizzled out leaving a cloud of ash in their stead. The quick ones vanished off into the night.

In moments, they had fled the area. The car leveled out quickly after that.

No one spoke for a minute, when Maddy chimed in.

"So, uh…what the fuck were those?" "A mere nuisance in the grand scheme out here. Push through, make haste," Jolt said right back over the radio to her.

With the lights on, we increased our pace, we could see what was coming ahead of us, but they would be able to see us too for miles away. What we didn't see were the demons far off in the distance.

Something crashed across the roadway in front of us, it vanished just as soon as it landed. Then we saw another one shortly after it. I peered into the distant night and saw a large silhouette in the dark night.

"Incoming!" Terra shouted out and pointed at something hurdling towards us in the air.

I tried jerking the wheel, but the initial damage couldn't be avoided. The car lurched, but far too late.

Basketball sized chunks of concrete collided with us. The rear passenger fender took a massive shot, the van sustained a hole ripped in the side of it moments after we heard the first impact.

"Fucking hell."

Maddy cursed audibly over the radio to Rachel. "Seal it," she shouted.

"I'm trying you asshole!" Rachel snapped at Maddy loudly.

Concrete projectiles flashed in my view and smashed on the road near us. I could tell they were ripped up from the ground or the freeway because they still had the iron bars jutting out from each side. A bright flash was all I could see before the possible impact.

"Back off a bit, we're less likely to take a hit if we're spread out." I communicated to Maddy through Jolt.

In answer, the van slowed, giving us a few car links of distance.

Maddy swerved all over the road after me. Every turn barely enough to avoid fatal impacts.

Each explosion sprayed the car with debris. Small stones and pebbles pattered down and over the top of the car, the sound like hail on a tin rooftop. A huge meteor of concrete collided with the front of Pearl and it took out the passenger headlight.

"Shit," Terra said holding onto the dashboard. He rocked back with the impact. The car met the stone and I saw the fender crush in before my head smacked the steering wheel. Blood poured down my face. All this technology available, and she couldn't have put an airbag in here? It felt like the tire avoided the damage at least, but Pearl had officially become a pirate now. I wasn't sure where I could get a car sized eyepatch at these hours. I wiped my forehead and continued to dodge projectiles.

"Hahahahahaha" Maddy laughed maniacally as she continued to swerve all over the road.

Then suddenly it stopped.

The hail of gigantic stones let up just as fast as they had started, I guessed we were out of that trap for now. We drove for a solid twenty minutes before something else made its way to us.

"Fuck," I said out loud again as I wiped the blood from my forehead. The wound healed up quickly, but I was a mess again. I blinked away blood that had dripped into my eyes as I drove further into this danger zone. The lights in the distance grew slightly nearer.

"WATCH IT!" Jolt shouted and I cut the wheel instinctively. Maddy followed suit. I looked in the rearview mirror to see a gaping chasm in the ground behind us. A pit of black nothing-ness. The yawning aperture in the ground looked like a sinkhole. Probably the home of a leviathan of sorts. Glad we had not seen one of those yet.

"Nice reflexes!" Jolt added.

That could've been it.

A long drop to a sea of demons. Not the best way to go.

"I could've made that," Maddy said cheerfully. "We could have jumped that right?"

"You're an idiot." Rachel chimed in from the background on the radio.

"Fuck you, just fix that hole." Maddy chided.

"I already sealed it," Rachel said over the radio. "Patched it up with some metal bits I took from the garage."

"Fuck me! You're like that old guy on TV, Macguvner, or whatever." Maddy fumbled with the name.

"MacGyver?" Rachel said.

"Yeah, that guy!" Maddy chortled.

Our passing moment of normality ended too soon.

The ground quaked beneath us. An enormous silhouette charged toward us from a home we were passing... Whatever had lived in that hole made its presence known.

Each step thundered, shaking the roadway. As he spanned into the distance of our rear lights, I saw its large gnarled hook hands. Its long arms dragged and scraped through the road behind us, destroying everything it ran through.

"Khadim?" Maddy asked. "Khadim, y-you see the huge ass demon too right?"

"I see it," I told her.

"Oh good, I thought I might be losing it," she replied.

"Got a plan?" Terra asked me.

"Nope," I said. "Not a clue."

If he caught up to us, we wouldn't be able to turn around and go back, the roadway was far too easily decimated by the monstrosity. A large mouth covered most of his face, enormous rows of teeth lined the top, and massive canines protruded through the bottom. I didn't see any eyes, but that didn't mean he couldn't see us.

He ran with gigantic loping strides on two pillar sized legs, like an ostrich might have. His head leaned out fully as his claws sprayed the earth high in the air behind him. Viscous slime oozed from his mouth and flew off in great streams behind him. He looked like a dog eyeballing a prime rib. All of his frightening details became clearer as he gained on us. Racing along at eighty miles an hour, we couldn't gain any ground.

Terra looked back with determination in his hazel eyes at the gigantic ominous creature. He spoke in a confident voice. "I got this, just stay steady," he said as he went to work.

He calmly rolled down the window and stuck his right hand out. I kept driving as the large demon blindly charged after us, and gained precious ground step by step. It howled a soul shaking melody that made my skin prickle.

"Maddy get in front of us." Terra said as he hung out of the window.

The van's engine thunder as she floored it and zoomed past us. She looked over at us with a wink as she passed, her cigarette dangling out of her mouth and her arm hanging out of the open window. Calm as a cucumber. A far stretch from the girl I first met who wanted to guide me away from danger, here we are smack dab in the worst of it together. The van's tail lights crested in front of us as she drove. We were coasting luckily; I'd picked up the pace to about ninety miles an hour right now.

"Maddy is in place in front of us." I told him, but I think he already knew it, because he leaned further out of the car and I felt Pearl jerk and tilt towards the passenger side momentarily. He began to pluck large chunks of road and hurl them at the demon, a similar tactic used on us by the unseen demons earlier. Each time he ripped up a new projectile to throw, the car would shift for a second. I could see them flash bright red by the taillights and then vanish into the distance. I knew when he landed his shots, I could hear the gurgling cry of the demon's rage. It leapt over the holes created by Terra and charged onward deftly maneuvering around the makeshift weapons. Leaning forward, it increased its speed. The ever-tenacious Terra continued to grab earth and hurl whatever he could get at the pursuant. In the rearview mirror, I saw a two-foot wall of stone pop up behind us, it ran in a straight line after the car. The demon crashed through it without much effort. The concrete roadblocks blasted down as fast as Terra could put them up.

"You got this Terra." I could hear Maddy over the radio.

I swerved through abandoned cars and other debris that littered the road, trying my hardest to maintain some sort of semblance of steadiness for Terra.

The massive demon continued to close the gap, now only a few hundred feet behind us. The car shook up and down as he neared. The tires barked. Pearl bucked against up and down against her will. Small tremors replaced jarring shifts in the roadways. The large demon seemed to have matched our pace, unable to catch us yet. "Damn it." Terra leaned back inside for a second and undid his seatbelt. I could already imagine Patty hitting him and telling him to buckle back up.

His face curled up into a mask of anger. His hazel eyes locked into mine with determination and frustration.

"I need you to stop the car." He scowled at me. "But Jolt said not to…" I implored.

"This is the only way to stop this thing!" he yelled and turned to the open window, bracing himself against the door.

If he wasn't so damned pure I swear.

I plunged my boot into the floorboard. The car protested and fishtailed all over the road. Our tires squealed and kicked up smoke. The driver side back left tire burst open causing the car to careen outwards in an arc to the right.

Terra came face to face with the monstrosity. We coasted to a stop and Terra stepped out of the car and dug his hands into the asphalt. The ground quaked as an immense black spear erupted from the ground in the distance and shot straight into the demon's path.

It persevered regardless, either it did not care about the barbed protrusion, or it couldn't move from its path.

The ground shook as the demon neared the spike on its path towards us.

BOOM

BOOM

BOOM

BOOM

BOOM

BOOM

The tempo pulsed as the demon thundered forward. A loud shriek escaped its cavernous maw.

The car rocked up and down as we sat and watched the oncoming Leviathan.

The car vibrated as the tire repaired itself. I didn't spare a single glance to see how it worked, I was far too worried about the gigantic monstrosity barreling its way towards us. Thank goodness for Patty and her contingency plans though, we would have been ground to a pulp if not for her engineering prowess. Even if she did miss the airbag thing earlier.

Terra waved his hand in a forward motion at me. "Go." He leaned back into the car grinning. He snapped his seatbelt on and stared into the rearview mirror drumming his hands on his thighs excitedly.

I punched it and the car lurched, our heads snapped back into our seats. More smoked poured from the tires. The demon plunged into the spear and it forced a deep hole through his chest. Black ichor dripped down its distended belly and onto the spear. The demons massive weight and momentum was far too much for the structure and the weapon snapped in half. The demon stumbled, fell, and continued to slide our way at a blazing speed. The road kicked up everywhere as we watched helplessly.

"No way we are getting out of this," I said as my knuckles turned white. "Shit. Shit. Shit." I hit the steering wheel with my fist. The car seemed to stand still as the demon slid closer and closer.

Terra shifted in his seat and leaned out of the window again as the demon hit us. The demon's body struck the rear passenger side fender. Under his daunting weight, we popped up into the air and hurled upwards. The view of the ground changed to the underbelly of Yggdrasil. We were going to plummet to our demise, and the demons would finish what the impact did not. If the Leviathan didn't get us, it would be the other carrion crawler demons that waited patiently in the shadows.

Out of the corner of my eye I spotted Terra leaning out the window and pulling at something like a rope.

The car leveled out and we rolled down to the surface with a bounce.

A bounce, not an explosion, or a sudden fatal crash. A mere thud was the most damage sustained. Terra guided the earth beneath the car like a wave, he pulled and pushed his arms out and guided us to safety. He stood like a sorcerer might as he cast his spells around widely.

The ground rose up and eased us down towards the road. Amazing and terrifying, something I'd gotten used to - almost.

Maddy watched us through gaping eyes as we pulled up past her on the road. Her cigarette fell out of her mouth and into the night. We left the demon to lick its wounds and pressed onwards.

I turned my attention to the road. I didn't need the goggles to show me the city now. The lights flickered for miles ahead of us, glowing brightly in the desolate wastes.

It seemed that all the demons that we had encountered had vanished. They receded into the body of the night, unable or unwilling to near the lights set out on the walls ahead. So they fell back to prepare for the next potential victims to happen through.

The light of the city shone like a beacon of hope, like a lighthouse guiding ships to shore, we knew where we were headed. Our car landed down onto ground level. Terra sat down again and leaned forward in his seat, grinning at me. He sported that proud grin of when you know you did something good. I smiled at him and clapped him on his shoulder.

"Saying I'm impressed would be an understatement, saying you have the biggest balls of anyone I've ever encountered might be closer to what I'm trying to convey." I told him.

All above us the spinning city quietly made its circuit.

"It's easy driving from here, we're only ten minutes out." Jolt said over the radio for everyone to hear.

"Nice job on that demon Terra." Jolt added.

"Bummer, I was hoping to run through something terrifying." Maddy smarted through the radio.

"You could turn around and go back if you want, just drop me off first!" Rachel said in an annoyed tone over the radio.

"They get to have all the fun." Maddy complained. "I want to ride on a concrete wave, just once."

CHAPTER 15
THE BURBS

As we approached the gates of the city, it seemed like they spread out over miles and miles. The first one we encountered gave off an enormous amount of light for a few thousand feet. The city above illuminated our path, but the lights coming off the wall seemed different than halogen bulbs. We gazed at the lamps, flames burned white hot inside of them. They put off heat as well, massive heat from this distance. Terra noticed my stare.

"It's holy fire, it keeps the demons back from the walls," Terra said.I nodded, I was beyond doubting something like holy fire now. "What about inside the city? Has there ever been a break in?" I pointed at the top of the wall.

"Mmmm…Not very often, occasionally something will dig its way through the earth to come up into the city unperturbed by the lights, they really only protect the outer walls. Nothing can break through these walls or barriers. Not that I've ever seen anyways. That Leviathan would be hard pressed to burst through the wall." He nodded at the massive structure in front of us.

"I imagine when you have architecture of this variety, a lot of contingencies go into place, but to set up an underground defense would be difficult without unearthing the entire city and placing a concrete floor that was even close to the size of these walls below." I surmised out loud.

"Exactly, so you wall up the outside and protect it as best as you can." Terra said as he rolled a ball of dirt in his hands.

The base would have to be done by Terra, and that task seemed unrealistic, even by his standards. The gates had no one around them, not an officer, teller, or clerk. I guess I expected someone official there.

"Guess security isn't necessary here?" I suggested.

"Seems like it." Maddy chimed in over the speaker.

We pulled up and let our vehicles idle while we figured out what to do next. I looked at Terra and then back outside. The gates towered above us, the color of white shimmering pearl. The thick bars seemed to go up forever.

Jolt had said they were made of a single pearl. That seemed a bit farfetched, so I didn't imagine it to be true, but my penchant for knowing things lately seemed questionable at best.

Jolt commented right on cue.

"Pearls from Heaven, dropped here, and forged by angels or so we're taught to believe. Faith can be trying at times. Yet, one thing you can believe in, is the J-man." He smiled wide in the monitor. "I always provide."

I heard a rumbling ahead and the gate shifted upwards in front of us, it took a few minutes to reach its apex, though it provided adequate room for us to drive underneath it.

I sat and watched it move upwards. The massive gate, a singular pearl the size of a building, crept up higher. I still couldn't believe it, even when I sat there and stared at it in person. The color shimmered a stunning white with a slight sheen over the top of it."What's the matter?" Terra asked when I didn't move right away.I stayed silent and drove underneath it to the other side. It occurred to me that once we were inside, we wouldn't be making our way out anytime soon, which troubled me a bit. I wasn't a fan of prisons. I truly hoped it would be more accommodating. Turning to Terra, I acknowledged his question.

"Nothing really, just considering everything that has been happening lately. That, and what exactly we're heading in to." I told him.

"I never thought I'd get to see the inside of this place," Maddy said. "So far, it's just as spooky as the outside."

"It gets better," Terra said shifting in his seat. "We're just on the outskirts of the city, remember we have a few hours of driving until we get to Yggdrasil." He pointed ahead. "That's the base, way in the distance." I turned and saw what he pointed at, it was the thick base that supported the spinning dish above us. It would've been difficult to miss.

We pushed on.

The roads were certainly better, well maintained with fresh asphalt. Streetlights lined the roads, helping us to see better. We passed various small shops along the way. Electric street signs showed up intermittently. One let us know that we would be passing into Saint Sandoval in twelve miles. I turned to Terra and gave him a questioning glance.

Terra grinned at this.

"It's a small town in between here and there. That's all, you're too paranoid. Have faith man." He shrugged as if we hadn't just fled from a gigantic demon and his pals. I'd had a hard time trusting in faith the last few years.Our adventure had taken a sharp turn from chaos and turned right into a family road trip. Taking in the sights as we went, we were sure to come upon the world's largest ball of yarn or something equally as ludicrous at some point. Sure enough, in place of the yarn, we passed by hundred-foot-tall angelic marble statues in varying poses. There were three within a five-mile stretch.

They varied in the clothing they wore, but each had the same hooded appearance that covered their eyes, the lips of each slightly agape, and all of them had a hand extended into a pointing gesture. Each one pointed to the same direction.

"They're pointing at the tree of life, Yggdrasil," Maddy said. "I heard about this from a guy that I met in Abysm. He said that you follow the angels if you wanted to get to the Tree of Life." She spoke in a matter of fact tone. "They're all over Ouroboros in different areas."

How the hell could you miss it?

"Never thought I'd get here." She reiterated her statement from earlier.

I watched as a town crested over the hill.

We drove into Saint Sandoval. A bright luminescent sign featured a man dressed in a priest's garb with a stein of beer in his hand. His electric hand waved back and forth at the road. It looked like one of those old drug store clowns that would turn and wave over and over, or one those giant puppets at the kids' pizza places. "That's fucking weird." Maddy chimed in over the radio.

Another sign, not too far behind the moving Saint said, *Gas next exit.* "No way," I said, still not believing a place like this existed. It seemed so calm here, nothing like our previous landscape filled with demons.

"Yep, and I would suggest filling up," Jolt said. I noticed the gas gauge teetered on empty. Pearl could run over demons and sustain massive damage, but fuel efficiency wouldn't be listed on the sticker for sure. I laughed at the thought of a tiny smart car trying to make it through all the shit we'd been through so far.

"You ok?" Terra asked when he saw me laugh.

"Yeah, I'm good." I told him.

I didn't understand how such a place existed , but I turned off onto the next exit and spotted a glowing building in the night, a large filling station with about sixteen pumps in a large concrete area. A couple other cars sat at the pumps, though I didn't see anyone with them. The sign out front read, Sanctuary, with a little halo around the S. The station had its prices out front like the traditional gas stations I remembered. Cheap too, only a few partials per gallon. Wasn't gas supposed to be a rarity?

I guessed it was possible that in the darkness, gas could be plentiful. Perhaps once inside, people didn't want to leave again, so they never bought any.

Beyond the pumps sat a store with lights that glowed brightly on the inside. I could see aisles lined with snack food, refrigerators filled with sodas, and neon signs humming in the windows. I felt like we had gone back to the time when the world hadn't been destroyed, and we were simply on a fun trip to the lake.

I pulled up next to pump two, and Maddy followed suit behind me at three. I stood up and shoved the damaged door out. It groaned, but opened with only minor protestations.

Terra got out and stood up, throwing his arms in the air to stretch. I looked back and saw Maddy step outside of the van. She pulled out a new pack of cigarettes and packed them in her palm as Rachel took a short stretch and walked over to us.

"The girl can drive; I'll give her that much credit." Rachel motioned with her chin to Maddy. "However, she's about two clowns short of a circus." She shared a warm chuckle with us.

"We got here in one piece, there's a lot to be said for that," Terra mentioned as he watched Maddy pack her smokes.

"The Constant is in one piece too, with his powers manifesting as well," Rachel said, grinning at me. Terra shot her a damning glance.

"Just saying, you're learning to control those powers of yours, right Constant?" She looked up at me encouraging my agreement.

"Khadim," I told her.

"Khadim," she said. Her lips curled up into a smile again.

Terra coughed loudly.

"I do think that I'm getting a better idea of how to control it," I said, turning my hands over in front of me.I nodded as I looked at them. I didn't get all of it, but I'd learned somewhat how to control these abilities. Not that I knew what I was supposed to properly do with them. Let's be honest, how many metal doors would I have to stick my hands through ever? I guessed I could use the heat to cook for myself, but I only ate for the taste of it. I didn't feel like I needed anything to sustain myself.

It took me a moment to realize it, but I enjoyed being able to get out of a car and stand up in the cool night air without getting sand blasted. My body could finally breathe without being stifled by a harsh environment. It even smelled fresh outside, aside from the gas fumes that permeated the air.

This was my first taste of normalcy, even though it might have been the most out of sorts area we had been to yet in our journey.

I took the goggles off and rubbed my eyes, sand had caked itself against my face and crumbled off in small packs. I stood there and shook the sand from my hair, whipping it back and forth as dust flung everywhere. Rachel tittered, but I didn't mind. I dusted off my clothing last, watching as the sand blew away in the brisk night breeze.

Terra stood back watching, he shook his head and laughed.

"Want a fun fact?" Terra said as he looked on. "When we get to Yggdrasil, you'll be able to take a shower, like a real one with soap even."

"God, I could use one of those right now." Rachel chimed in.

I could almost feel the hot water soothing my skin, the pressure would feel so good. I'd been dreaming about a shower since I got to the Deep Diner, I would even pay all of my eleven dollars to someone *just* to take a shower.

In fact, the promise of warm water cleansing my body almost justified the entire journey. Lying on a gurney for who knew how long, in a room that smelled like raw meat, going on a journey through endless gusts of sand, covered in who knew what kinds of filth, for God knows how many days. A shower might make me forget all that shit ever happened.

I felt a genuine grin spread across my face.

"I know, right?" Terra said, grinning back at me.

"Wow, he does smile!" Rachel laughed.

Maddy slid over to me with an unlit cigarette in her mouth. She looked at Terra and me. "Did you guys find a piece of candy in your pocket or something?"

She huffed out a small chuckle and got back to her original thought.

"Hey Khadim, could you give me one of those dollars that you found?" She held her hand out. "I want to go blow it in there." She leaned back towards the shop. "Do you have any clue, how long it's been since I've been to a proper convenience store? I'm hoping they have an Icee machine, oh man, the cherry bomb flavors!" She reminded me of a kid. "Come on man! Just a buck! I won't spend it all."

I laughed and pulled the wallet out of my back pocket. I handed her a wrinkled dollar bill, covered in sand. She took it and shook it off.

"I'll be back," she said as she bolted off towards the store, cigarette bobbing up and down as she ran.

Rachel walked over to something on the side near the grass. It looked like an old phone booth.

"I'll get gas," Terra said pointing to the pump.

I nodded without looking at him, and watched Rachel place some coins in the phone. She began talking on the phone with an unknown person. She nodded her head and looked up and made eye contact with me.

Pulling her hair back over her ear, she smiled. I watched in wonder as she turned her back to me to face the phone booth. I could see the small of her back when she stretched upwards, he muscles taut and her skin covered in goosebumps. She placed her right hand on the top of the booth, and raised her hands in a shrug before hanging the phone back on its base. Without a glance, she turned and headed inside the store as well. Still a bit of a mystery that one.

I heard talking come from behind me, like a tinny voice from a shitty speaker. "In local news, the Peters beat the Jobs, three to two today. Colin Smecker hit a walk off homerun in the eleventh inning." Terra stood watching the monitor on the gas pump. I walked up behind him and watched on as well.

"The drama continues on Walking for Cash," a commercial showed twelve people walking down a roadway in the sunlight. "Rusty Bader, local favorite from Saint Sandoval was gunned down after taking a fall during the race. After his third warning, he leaned back and laid on the road until he was shot." The commercial stopped.

Terra looked up at me out of his daze. "The car's full." He looked surprised. He unplugged the fuel nozzle and placed it back on the pump station.

"You're telling me that they have sports and reality television here?" I asked him, still staring at the screen that now sat blank.

He looked embarrassed, "Yeah. It's...something to keep people occupied instead of trying to leave, I guess." He smiled and shifted his shoulders nervously. "I actually enjoy baseball, since it's the only sport that's on anymore." He shrugged. "The Peters are my favorite team. They're all biblical names." I shook my head at that, this place was like a Christian theme park.

I thought it was pitiful that after the world fell apart, things like sports and reality television still went on. Did the masses not even see what happened to the world? Entertainment was just a luxurious crux created for the idle mind. Too much to be fixed out there to sit back watching television.

"What are the requirements to live here?" I asked him out of curiosity.

"Wealth and connections," he answered quickly. "Sometimes dumb luck, there are homeless communities of people who managed to sneak past the gate somehow." He explained as he leaned on the car. "They have shelter, food, water, and television. They stay in their home and watch TV, keeps them from being on the street causing trouble." He smiled with a shrug.

The fact that he considered these people to be a nuisance was a bit of shock from someone with such a clean aura. Like television could be the only answer to keep these people numb to the outside world.

Terra continued.

"This is one of several communities in the area in fact, each town is different, but we're all hooked up to the same feeds." He pulled excess dust from Pearl and guided it into the trashcan. "You know your boy Jolt there is the one who provides the shows and feeds hooked up into every single home along the way."

That information did not sit well with me. I definitely needed to keep the goggles off me.

"That's why he has a home in the desert and is protected from other virtues, so long as he keeps the feed going with shows. He even directs each one," Terra told me as he cleaned the car's windshield. "He's almost everywhere, well the shows are anyways." As he said this, the monitor on the pump flashed on and off.

"He's basically off limits to everyone," Terra stated as he walked to the store. "We should get the girls and go seek Solace."

"Wait, who would come after Jolt? I thought he was a Virtue? Aren't you guys supposed to be like mutants or something?" I asked him as I thought of the old comics I used to read.

"No, just off limits I guess. No one ever challenges him over anything. Heh, mutants…" he shrugged and continued towards the store.

I had more questions by the minute. I decided the goggles would stay off me for a while, that was way too much power. One person shouldn't be able to control what everyone saw. Free will should come to the people on their own. If you blotted out the thinking process, you limited what they were capable of.

I walked with Terra into the store and glanced at the young woman in her late

teens standing behind the counter. She watched a monitor that had a game show on. "Which box?" The monitor screamed loudly. The crowd shouted out different numbers and the host informed the contestant they only had one shot to get it right. "Hey!" Maddy walked up to me from the innards of the store.

She got right in my face and leaned in my ear. "This place is fucking weird, right?" She whispered so that only I could hear her. "I mean, what's with all the televisions? This chick has been staring at the screen since I walked inside, not even a fucking hello. They're on every fridge too." She pointed over at the glass doors lining the walls with cold drinks.

"They even have little monitors all along the snack shelves." She opened her eyes wide at me and motioned at them. "WEIRD."

I looked around and saw the monitors. They were everywhere, you couldn't turn your head without seeing one. Maddy followed my eyes around. She had an enormous cup filled with some red liquid, it had freshly formed frost on the outside of the cup. Like the contents were ice cold. She carried about four or five small bags in her other hand. Different varieties of snacks, chips, candy, etc. Maddy looked at me with a "don't judge me" face.

"Wanna see something else fucked up?" Maddy asked me while chewing on licorice.

"Check this shit out." She walked over to a water fountain and pressed the handle in with her hip. Water came shooting out of the hole. She just stood there holding it and the water continued to pour out and vanish down the drain. She looked at the water and then at me, then back to the water. Her eyes grew wide, her long eyelashes fluttered over her emerald lenses staring at me in silence. I think she was waiting on me to respond.

"I don't get it," I said.

"Water," she said. "*Free* water! What the actual fuck?!"

She put her hands up in the air, with a wide-eyed look. "No one gives away free water! I also know that the water on this side was fucking poisoned by Satan." she said, nodding her head enthusiastically. The monitors through the shop flickered on and off. The place started to become too much for me, I felt dizzy.

I grabbed her by the arm and stomped over to the counter where the girl stood watching the monitor. The volume was far too loud. That dull ache in my head swelled.

"OH. I'm so sorry Hannah. It seems that the box *you* chose, only has a one-way trip to the Outlands," the host said. The clerk chortled gleefully and clapped her hands at the monitor.

Maddy cleared her throat loudly. "MMHMM." She exaggerated loudly.

The girl behind the counter turned and looked at Maddy for the first time, breaking her trance. "Yes, welcome to Sanctuary where we have all the necessities to accommodate your needs." She gave a woeful smile that seemed forced. Her pallid features lax from hours of endless television.

Maddy placed her drink and snacks on the counter. "This," she said, motioning to the items with a wave.

The girl looked up at her and then over at me with her tired aqua eyes. "Is she with you Constant?" I furrowed my brow, but nodded. How the hell did this girl know I was the Constant? Oh god, now I was calling myself the Constant.

"It's all free of charge." She smiled, this time much worse than before.. She strained a grin that crinkled her nose up. "Courtesy of Solace, our beacon of hope," she droned.

Maddy opened her eyes wide, tilted her head, turned to me,

and gave me a firmly lifted left eyebrow. It was her "What the fuck?" glance.

She scooped her goods from the counter and walked outside.

Rachel walked out from the bathroom and looked up to see me standing there watching Maddy walk out. She blushed, and wiped her hands on her pants.

"I don't think I could've gone another mile without bursting." She grinned, walking toward the girl behind the counter. The girl, of course, had already returned to her monitor.

Rachel knocked her knuckles on the counter and the clerk turned to make eye contact. "Yes, welcome to Sanctuary where we have all the necessities to accommodate your needs."

Rachel said, "That's better. Pump three." She motioned outside to the van. "Fill her up."

The girl looked at me again for approval before flipping a switch and pressing a button. "Take what you need Constant." She then turned back to the monitor.

Rachel gave me a sidelong glance. I raised my hands up at a loss.

"Does that mean I can get something to drink while we're here?" Terra said from behind us.

"I guess so, if not, I have money," I said to him.

Both Rachel and Terra walked over to the refrigerated section and the monitors kicked on at each door. "Tune in as we see the Davids battle the Goliaths on Tuesday!" Old organ music played baseball tunes in the background. The monitors turned off each time the doors opened and closed. I watched from the middle of the store as the doors opened, and the monitor moved to the inside of the refrigerator, then back to the front as the door shut.

Rachel and Terra both walked over with a bottle of water. The clerk continued to ignore us. She stared at the screen as another cheer went up and giggled aloud again.

We hauled our food and drinks back to the car where Maddy

stood, pumping gas into the van. She bounced up and down at the knees, a piece of licorice hanging from her mouth and her cigarette resting behind her heavily pierced ear. She hummed some thrumming beat.

I noticed her light blonde hair had grown in a little bit since we had first met. She was kind of cute under that tough exterior. I grinned at her, she nodded at me in acknowledgement. The cigarette sat still as she looked over at me. She drank with the straw in her mouth next to the licorice. Sucking down the red drink too quickly, she grabbed her head after a few seconds. I understood that pain, my head was still aching from everything that just happened in the gas station.

As we were standing there waiting to for the tank to fill , a black limousine pulled into the parking lot. They parked over by the sign and the driver's door opened. Out stepped a full-sized gorilla, dressed in a suit. See, I knew this gorilla, this was not a phrase I would have ever thought I'd use, but it worked in that strange situation. That gorilla had sat at the front of Jolt's home. He walked on his knuckles and back legs to the rear door of the limo. When he placed a large hand, and opened the door, I didn't even have to guess who it would be. Out of the car came Jolt, his arms open wide as he sauntered over to us.

"My man!" He said extending an embrace. I blankly took the hug and looked over as the gorilla closed his door and went still.

"I thought you were back in the desert?" I asked him as he backed up a bit from the embrace.

"No, no, that's only part me." He grinned that wide grin of his. "I have outlying cells that act for me. Robots. Dig?" He gestured wide and turned left and right. "This, is me in the flesh. Can't be out in that heat, it's bad for my skin!"

He stood there wearing sunglasses in the middle of the night. "The peepers are for my astigmatism, plus, I hate bright lights." He gave a *what can you do* smirk and a giggle. I looked him over, one hundred percent a robot, and it clearly had no aura. I just played along with him though. "Now, if you'll come with me. I'll take you to Solace. She's patiently waiting for you." He placed his arms out in front of him towards the open door.

I looked over at my companions who had gathered around us. I could hear as Maddy slurped the remainder of her Icee.

"I'll take good care of those cars, don't you worry none my friend," Jolt said. He tilted his head to the left. "Rachel, you take the van." She looked at Maddy, so did Jolt. "You my fine lady, will be coming with us," Jolt said as he offered her a hand. Maddy looked repulsed as she furrowed her thick eyebrows.

"If there's one thing I've learned from being in Khadim's mind it's that he doesn't go anywhere without you." He smirked as he retracted his hand. Maddy reached into her pockets and handed the keys to Rachel. She then walked over to the trash can and hurled the empty cup into it. When she returned, she only had her purse and the bag of licorice with her. "If I eat all that shit I bought right now, I am going to puke. I'm already done with sugar after just getting it again." She placed the rest of the licorice in her purse and pulled the cigarette from behind her ear and placed it in her mouth. When she did this, the gorilla came over with a lighter and placed it in front of her. Maddy jumped, but with a wary glance, she used the flame to light her smoke. The gorilla backed up and stood still next to the car again.

"You have more of them?" She blew a stream of smoke from her mouth and asked about the gorilla. She played with the lapels on the animal's coat.

"Many more! They took to the robot engineering much quicker than my doubles did." He stood tall and turned his attention to Terra. "You, my earthy friend will be driving Pearl to the garage. She'll need repairs." Terra nodded compliantly at Jolt.

Terra held out his hand to me, and I tossed him the keys. I trusted him to take care of the car since he knew Patty. I hoped that she'd still be ok with all the trouble that I started when I ran out in the Abysm. I didn't have to worry about Faul making his way in to get her, though. That comforted me at least, the Glass fellow sounded like trouble, but maybe Patty could deal with him in her own way. I would have to go back sometime soon and check up on her.

I looked at the limo and at Jolt and wondered if he was ever *not* watching. It bothered me that he saw everything. He said that he dealt in information, like a human processing machine. Always watching and taking in information, his robots sorted the data for him. I wondered how humane that could be. He ran all the shows, and information into everyone's homes. If this place was half as massive as I had been told it was, that was millions and millions of people being fed whatever he wanted them to see.

He obviously had some kind of deal with Solace, and that immediately made me worry about her mindset. People seemed to praise her here like a holy figure. The girl at the gas station sure did. Were all the people around here going to be drones like the clerk? I could only hope it was limited to a small portion of them.

Jolt raised an eyebrow. "I can see you are thinking deeply about something, but we cannot stand on ceremony here. I worry that Solace may in fact become impatient, and no one wants that."

I seriously doubted she didn't know what was going on. More than likely she was watching us through this robot, or whatever monitors were nearby. I'm not sure what I had gotten myself and Maddy into. I just kept thinking about that shower, I needed something to hope for.

The gorilla opened the door to the limo, and Maddy and I climbed in. Jolt said something else to Rachel and Terra then he joined us inside.

CHAPTER 16
A CHAT WITH JOHNNY JOLT

We sat down in the back of the limo, and Jolt took a seat on the opposite side of us. Dressed in a black suit with a yellow lightning bolt that stretched down his arm, he leaned back with his arms across the back of the seat his hands covered in those silky golden gloves. As the limo began to pull forward, he laughed in relief. "Ah Khadim, I didn't think you would make it this far." He grinned. "Getting you through that shit show took effort. Demons, that big oaf Faul, Avery, and now the dark. I'm exhausted just talking about it." He chortled gaily. Jolt squinted through his glasses, his eyebrows told me he had some thoughts on our adventure so far. "It's always a bit blurry at first, but you have been out for a fair amount of time already. Not to mention you killed Faul. Which is something that we certainly hadn't planned for." He sighed and shrugged. "C'est la vie."

I looked up at him. "Why shouldn't I have killed Faul? He came after me, and almost killed Terra? That Avery guy too. They both wanted to kill me." I added.

"Faul wanted you dead, Avery wanted you in a different way, to be a part of his entourage or something." He countered me, stroking his chin. He sat up and leaned on his knees.

"Faul has always been a terror. He first showed his gigantic misshapen head here twenty years ago. He was around for the long haul. He even decided to keep the Outlands to himself and no one argued with him, big idiot always thought he knew what was best. Would you want that shithole? So, he created all the different gangs to run it for him while he got drunk in Abysm for years, I'd hate to see his actual tab, could you imagine the sheer amount of liquor it would take to inundate that fool?"

"Wait." Maddy chimed in. "Ever since I could remember, he was just the leader of the Shavs, but no one would mess with him, just because he was so…"

"Violent?" Jolt tilted his hand out.

"Yeah. I mean I had heard about people flayed in the desert and left to cook in the sunlight," she said with a look of horror on her face. "At Abysm, he had his own way of killing people, he would tie people to chains on the ground, while he stood at the top of the hill with a gigantic glass lens." She shook her head in disgust.

I thought about those glass bases we saw outside of Abysm.

"He would burn them like ants. The sun cooked them where they were chained." She finished her thought.

"Brutal," Jolt said, sitting forward as he listened intently. "Faul could be that way though, and we couldn't have this cozy place to ourselves if it wasn't for him." He surmised as he rolled his head back and around. "You take the bad with the good. Am I right Constant?" He stopped and looked right at me.

"No," I said, shaking my head. "You don't take the bad with the good. Both sides always manage to fuck it up with their own agendas. Never letting people just… be. Let them make their own mistakes without influencing them." The smile on his face faded into a grimace, the first of which I'd seen from him.

"You've got that wrong my friend. People are sheep, and they need to be herded." He shook a finger at me. "The good shepherd has arrived too." He gestured towards me.

He had finally shown his true colors. My own balance stood in peril in this half of the world.

He then leaned back again and put his arms out over the backs of the seats. The rest of the trip was silent.

Our limo sailed through the night, the barren roads a welcomed relief compared to the demon-filled streets from earlier. When we came to a checkpoint, the gate stood open, allowing us to pass through unabated. It seemed like the populace here had been divided up into different suburbs, each one under a different Saint's name. Saint Anthony. Saint Peter. Saint Donovan, and so on.

Each suburb we passed looked the same, each person was sealed up in their own comfortable way. The innards of each house were accompanied by the soft glow from televisions inside. The tenants no doubt sitting comfortably on a couch or in bed staring on at the mindless feeds provided by Jolt. No one walked outside as we passed, no movement on the streets. It made me question the cars I saw at Sanctuary earlier. Were they placed there as props to provide a feeling of normality?

I wondered to myself if people had ever gotten up to leave before? Did they succeed at getting out? Was this just a place to come and wait for your inevitable death? My thoughts shifted back to the present when Jolt spoke.

"The final leg of the tour," he said.

The last gate opened and we drove inside. This portion of the city, vastly different than the rest. All around us, I gazed upon vast churches, and enormous buildings lit up on the outside. There were large industrial buildings, lots full of steel, lumber, and stone. Workers buzzed around each area, taking shipments out of the gate and, presumably, into the towns beyond.

The freeway system broke off into many different routes. The road we drove along on must have been the main artery. It stretched for thirteen lanes, six going north, six going south, with the middle road segregated only for us. To either side of us stood barricades that housed us inside, like an HOV lane without an exit. If we crashed, the car would have to be lifted out to clear it. I don't know when we got into the center lane exactly, but I was sure it hadn't been too long ago. Perhaps after the last gate.

Jolt must have noticed my stare.

"Service lane. Only the big dogs get a pass in it." Jolt motioned to himself and at me. "Direct to the entrance, no stops in between, the quickest route possible, as the crow flies anyhow."

We drove in that lane for a few more miles, when the road split. The center lane continued onward, as the other two lanes ran off parallel to the walls. The center path had its own entrance at the end of a large cul-de-sac.

Fields of dying yellow grass surrounded us on either side, along with hills upon hills of rotten apples, decaying oranges, and many other fields of forlorn fruits. Clouds of buzzing flies swarmed among the fallen fruit.

Workers trudged through the hills and trampled rotten fruit as they went, pools of juice saturated the grounds beneath the hills, running into sewer grates below. Men in black with glowing flamethrowers burned the dead produce they passed. Men in the outskirts controlled the burn. Flies fled in droves into the air from one pile to the next. It was this way on both sides of us, all around the base of Yggdrasil. Droves of workers purged the endless fields of decaying fruit. "You must trim away the infection." Jolt said, shaking his head as he watched the workers. "Lest it be your demise."

The limo drove slowly around the cul-de-sac, the gorilla parked at the end of it near the base. The engine hummed softly in our ears, then died away as the car came to a standstill.

The gorilla got out and opened our door. Jolt stood on the opposite side of his robot ape. "This is where we part ways Constant. I assure you though, we will be in contact again sooner than later. Just keep an open mind about all of this will you?" he asked. "Or the shelter you live inside, could indeed collapse upon you."

I had just been warned.

We got out of the car and into the roadway. The smell of burning fruit, wasn't all that bad, fragrant for certain, but not a bad smell like the sulfur from the Outlands. I'd inhaled enough bad scents in the past to be sated. The smoke wafting nearby got siphoned up into the concrete sky above us. Open grates sucked the air through it.

When I looked up, I saw that the entire sky above us was covered by the building they called Yggdrasil. I watched as a mass of rotting pears fell earthward from a chute above and in the distance, other chutes allowed various fruit to fall. You could hear the splatter of them in the distance.

Maddy nudged my arm.

"Looks like they are ready to receive you, oh Constant." She motioned towards the doorway that had appeared. A slender silhouette stood there in the light. I turned again and watched the burning fields before turning back to Maddy.

As Jolt's limo drove away, Maddy leaned over to me again.

"You do realize that this is all sorts of fucked, right?"

I couldn't agree more.

CHAPTER 17

WE HAVE ARRIVED

WE WALKED TO the open doorway, where a woman stood, her hands placed on her hips, dressed in a white work coverall. Her statuesque figure, along with her head full of cognac ringlets and sapphire eyes, gave her an overwhelming presence of power. She shot us a smile that was both, confident and bold.

"Khadim." She turned. "Maddy." She placed her hands together and bowed. "It's so nice to meet you both. We've been waiting for you for a while. I'm Sloane, Solace's personal assistant.

She looked on expectantly, "We understand there were some... hiccups along the way and that you killed Faul, the Sun Virtue?" She looked down at my hands, inspecting them from a distance.

The gloves I wore were in shambles at this point, and I had kept them on more out of habit than anything else. I pulled them off and placed them in my pockets.

"Yes, he was kind of overbearing. When it came down to either myself surviving, and Terra possibly dying, the only option I had was to kill him, so both of us could live." I said in a sarcastic, but serious tone. Defending my decision to kill Faul was becoming tiresome. "Yet, Terra caused your car to crash, right?" The redhead asked with her inflection rising at the end of her sentence, as she plainly accused Terra.

I nodded, "He caused the accident, but he said that if not for the crash, he could not have helped me get here." I stroked my bearded chin, dust fell out of it and onto my jacket. The sand felt like a parasite that latched onto me for dear life. I wondered if she knew the way to the showers.

"He said that Solace sent him to help me." I thought about this last bit of information again. "He came there to make sure that Faul didn't impede my progress, or kill me I would imagine. So, to me, it seems like by Solace sending Terra to help me, she helped get Faul killed in the process. That, or she would have a dead kid on her hands, which no one wanted."

She nodded the whole time and wrote on her clipboard as she listened. "I see," she stooped and put her hand to her ear. She listened to someone, or something. She looked back up at Maddy and I and smiled.

"I'm also to understand that Maddy had a large part of how you know what might be going on somewhat? I mean to say the current affair of the world we live in."

I looked over at Maddy.

She turned her eyes to Sloane and answered for herself.

"He didn't really know much, a bit clueless really. Wandered off right into trouble. Fuckin idiot ran into a Shav, less than a mile into his walk." She laughed and pulled her earlobe, her mass of earrings jangled as she let go. "Not that the guy ended up being any sort of trouble. Khadim killed him and snatched his clothes up. It was better than what he was wearing from the other guy he killed when he woke up! He looked like a surfer! Can you imagine?" She chuckled loudly.

Sloane wrote everything down on her clipboard. She looked up from the keyboard and turned her sultry sapphire eyes back onto Maddy.

"The fact that he killed two people, for what appeared to be their clothing alone, didn't deter you from joining him on his journey?" She prodded Maddy.

Maddy laughed and then smiled, "He said I was good, and then we both found out that we hated butane lighters. I mean, I never got that from anyone else. Simple connections, I never thought I was 'bad,' but that didn't mean people didn't just treat me like a piece of meat. Khadim never dismissed me, he listened and actually processed what I said." She smirked at me. "Most of the time anyhow."

Maddy rubbed at the new light blonde hair on her head. "He just let me be me." She shrugged. "That shit never happens."

"I see." Sloane shook her head up and down and wrote more on her pad. All the while her hair bobbed up and down. She was very well kept, her hair was spotless and had hairspray in it. You could smell it. She looked up at me and placed her pen in her notes and shut the cover.

"Well, I'm not going to make you stand around down here all day." She turned and headed down the enormous concrete hallway in front of us. "This is Yggdrasil, the world's only building that can give you both night and day. It's on a twelve-hour rotation, so the balance is there, but the hours can be off a little bit for people who rely on the day for getting work done."

She pressed a button on the wall and a large doorway opened to show a rolling pathway. Sloane walked over and stepped onto it. We both followed her lead.

The walls whipped by as we stood still on this moving belt, propelling us further down the hallway expediently. "The building itself is filled with thousands of people. While our cities below encompass fourteen hundred miles roughly, Yggdrasil covers about half of that. We do, however, go about five and a half miles into the air. Yggdrasil is the largest structure ever created in the known world."

"Who sits at the top?" I asked, assuming I knew who it would be.

"No one." She grinned. "We believe it is bad luck to fill the top floor."

"Why?" I asked her.

"You should ask," she started.

"Solace, yeah-yeah." I finished her sentence for her.

It made me itch when people couldn't give me answers, it seemed like everyone went out of their way to make me question things. That summed up this society so far, it stifled what you knew so it could have the upper hand. Maddy became the only one who actively produced information for me. I didn't dare put my goggles on, in the off chance that Jolt would listen in. If they weren't so useful, I would've tossed them off the walkway for good.

He'd said if it wasn't a neurological connection, he couldn't get a reading anyhow. I had to believe that if I wanted some sort of privacy in my life.

The pathway turned and we zipped down another long hallway. The place seemed as if it was nothing more than a concrete palace. I looked around and saw some cracks in the wall where it looked like roots of a tree protruded through. Vines and leaves decorated the surface of dark brown bark.

We moved further and it went back to concrete. Varying roots protruded through the floor next to the moving walkway in many different areas. As if a massive tree was trying to break out of a prison.

"Could it be any fucking colder in here?" Maddy said aloud, rubbing her arms. "I might have to find some actual sleeves soon if so."

The temperature in the hallways teetered between cold and frosty. I imagined the insulation in there kept it as such.

"Seriously, I never thought I'd actually long for the Outlands heat," Maddy said as she shivered. Goosebumps littered her well-tanned skin.

I laughed.

"I just want to see something other than concrete." I told her. More vines protruded through the walls and floor as we went on for what seemed ages.

I felt as if I'd walked behind the walls at a football stadium, with doorways here or there that lead you to walk onto the field. I'm sure there were plenty of hidden rooms around, no way that it could just be solid concrete.

I wondered how long it took to build a place like that, what kind of hours? How many people came together and built it? Yggdrasil was probably on par with the Pyramids in Egypt with all of its what-ifs, I just rode the path until it finally came to an end.

When it did, I watched as Sloane ran off the end. Maddy did as well. I had to speed up to catch my balance. I imagined the amount of injuries people must have endured from riding that thing for the first time, it would really put a damper on your day. Angels and demons would pale in comparison to a severely sprained ankle. I smirked to myself.

When we stopped and looked around, there was nothing but more damned concrete everywhere. The only difference being a small opening to our left. Another hallway, though it lead inside rather than around the building. A middle aged Asian man, possibly in his mid to late forties, stood outside of the entrance, his frame, lean and lithe. He was near a table with many small plants, he walked around them trimming here and there. He would place his hand in the soil, and the plant seemed to get fuller.

When we turned down the hallway, I saw that there were many more roots that protruded from the ground, and the hallway itself filled with branches and leaves. Not much light came through the vast array of vines and branches. Lights provided a dim look at what might've been a dead end.

Sloane turned to us, and then to the man who tended the plants, she extended an arm out gesturing to him. "This is Minh, he guards our sole entrance to the top." She stuck her arm out and pointed down the hallway. "He is also a virtue."

He tittered gaily.

"I came with the tree," he said from the other side of the room to us.

Minh turned and ambled over to us, taking his time. He turned to Sloane and bowed low. He then bowed to Maddy. Lastly, he came over and extended a hand to me. I took his hand and shook it, as he placed his left hand on my wrist. He backed up then and spoke to us.

"I am Minh, it is so nice to meet you both." He had a light accent when he spoke, omitting the ends of many words.

"Constant, you are most welcome here." He grinned and motioned me over. I strolled toward him, leaving Maddy with Sloane. We roamed in front of a table featuring many varieties of plants. I was not someone very familiar with plants, but he had fruits, vegetables, and herbs all over.

The scents of basil and thyme danced on my senses. I looked and saw some glistening red tomatoes on a spiraling vines. I knew what those were because I despised raw tomatoes. However, in that moment, they were the most gorgeous things I'd seen. He giggled gaily as he watched me.

We walked further into the area where many tables were set with vastly different plants. It was truly amazing; my first sign of vegetation came from within a concrete room. The irony was not lost on me.

"Beautiful are they not?" he looked lovingly at a vine he held in his hand gently.

I nodded as I admired the bonsai trees and various flowers in bloom. They all smelled wonderful, floral scents were something I had forgotten about in my time in the new world. He watched as I enjoyed myself.

"They're amazing." I admitted to him as I stuck my nose in one taking in the sweet scent.

"Plants are my hobby," he said as he plucked an orange from a tree in the hallway and handed it to me. It smelled so sweet and perfect, I began to peel and eat it. The flavor sang out over my palate, it was easily the best orange I had ever had. Minh continued. "They are, in fact, my life. I spend endless days down here watching them grow, and tending to their individual needs. Plants need much care daily. They need to be trimmed when they're overgrown, or they can run rampant and destroy the other plants. They need to be watered, and have rich soil so that they may grow." He paused.

"Yet, when we humans did not exist, these plants did just fine on their own did they not?" He smiled and raised his eyebrows. "We as humans, say that we *must* do this, we *must* do that, or it won't work!" He made gestures for each point and giggled again.

I swallowed my orange and listened to him.

"Who is to say that man is truly in power over plants? Without us, they will flourish on their own, or be wiped out due to contagion. This is nature is it not?"

I considered his words and nodded.

"Nature has a natural homeostasis. No matter the weather, winds, rain, snow, or an overbearing sun. The world always tends to right itself. Even now with the world split in half, we have plants that grow here, and there are plants that thrive in the heat on the other side, whether on the surface or far below."

He smiled and looked up at the ceiling. A large root protruded from the wall. "Balance will always find its way." He giggled and smiled widely at me. His aura glowed bright green, which is something rare. He was almost at one with nature itself. Not a single sin in his aura. He and Terra were in an exclusive group.

Sloane cleared her throat.

Minh looked over to Sloane and bowed. "Apologies, please allow me to open the pathway." He took the orange peel from my hand and tossed it into a box of other peels and the like. He then ambled slowly into the hallway ahead, and Sloane came over to where I looked at the plants.

"I'm so sorry, he has been down here for years just talking to his plants, and he is kind of obsessed." She dismissed him with a shake of the head.

"Seems like he's happy to me." It also seemed like he and I were of a like mind. He settled more towards the middle of things than the others did. If he was a virtue, and going off what I'd learned, I was sun, he was plants, and Terra was earth, I don't think it was all that strange that we got along. Not that I actively chose to be sun, but the chips fell how they did. How serendipitous, as Terra would say.

Maddy came over to my side, chewing on a new piece of licorice.

"What did the plant dude say?" she asked between chews. "He looked like he was babbling a lot."

I smiled again. "He told me he was on our side."

"Ah." She swallowed her piece of licorice.

"What does that mean?" She whispered in my ear.

"Just means he's trying to find his balance too," I said quietly so Sloane didn't hear.

Maddy took one more piece of licorice and placed it in her mouth. She stuck the remainder in her bag.

I watched as Minh walked to the wall and placed his hand on the root jutting from the wall. He placed his other hand on the underside of it. The rest of the hallway started to shift and move. Plants receded into the wall, full blooms of flowers shrunk to pods, and eventually vanished as the roots shifted inside the concrete. The foliage all along the hallway diminished until you could see a bright light on the other side of the passage. Dry leaves crunched as we walked over them towards the growing light.

The air smelled so fresh, like we were standing in a forest. I didn't want to leave. I turned back, and Minh waved at us from the other side.

Maddy looked up at me. "Glad that dude is down here, I bet he keeps this place from careening over into the earth."

Solid point. "That's pretty much what he does." Sloane added. "He keeps the tree happy and maintains the balance within the building. Five and a half miles into the air gets really damn windy as you can imagine. He's the only one who can make the tree as strong as it is."

"You mean to tell me; this is an actual tree?" Maddy pointed at the ceiling.

"Have you been paying attention?" Sloane asked. "This is the World Tree, and some other architecture build onto it. A lot, of extra architecture."

Maddy looked annoyed. She chewed her licorice with vigor.

"I'm sorry, I didn't read my fucking pamphlet on the way in, not all of us have had the luxury of living in a place like this." Maddy snapped as she pointed at Sloane and then the walls with her soggy bit of licorice.

I thought about what Sloane said. They had built directly on to the World Tree. No wonder the tree was trying to get out of the concrete, damn thing was confined inside of it. What kind of egomaniac does that? I'd bet my eleven dollars I was going to get to meet her very soon.

Once we exited the hallway, the branches regrew to fill the hallway up tight. On this side of it, you could watch the roots wind their way together, a beautiful tapestry of nature. Roots formed taut cables that closed the exit tightly. I imagined Minh on the other side, going back to his plants and all the while, knowing he could bring this thing down as an afterthought if he so chose to.

We walked towards the elevator in the near distance. It waited with its doors open for us. The insides of it were golden, the floors a plush red velvet, and the panel had two pearl buttons that had the open and close signs on them. In a row of buttons labeled one to twelve, Sloane hit the twelve, a new screen popped up when she did this. It had the numbers zero to nine, she then hit the nine twice. At the top right, there was an icon that showed the floor you chose. It read, twelve hundred and ninety-nine.

The doors on the elevator slid shut, on the inside of the doorway we could see our reflection. Disheveled might almost describe my appearance. My black hair stuck out all over, my beard had grown, and continued to leave a trail of dust wherever I went. My aqua eyes looked tired but determined.

When the elevator began to move, the walls shifted into a translucent surface. All around us, we could see the innards of Yggdrasil.

"Wow." I couldn't help myself.

"This place is enormous," Maddy said as she echoed my thoughts.

"It never fails to give you a sense of awe," Sloane said as she peered out with us.

The floors opened wide in the center, the base being the widest, stretched on for endless miles. It seemed like this must be a special elevator, I could see many others all around falling far short of the top.

We could see people moving about here and there. Large, brightly lit signs in different languages littered the hallways. Seemed like Yggdrasil was a hub for all types. Perhaps survivors from all over the world came and congregated here for shelter. "We host all cultures, whoever wants to get in, and can afford it, of course." Sloane said matter-of-factly echoing my sentiments.

"Those who can't afford it?" I asked.

Sloane shrugged, "We all make it by our own means."

"So much for the virtuous," I said as I met eyes with Maddy. Sloane spun around to face me.

"Solace takes refugees to the outlying cities; this is the only pay to stay place around anymore. Most money is useless here, people pay in work, and fill various roles amongst the cities. This is how the outside few get inside. They work for it." She chided me. "It's not much of a cash system anymore Constant."

I stayed my questions. We were almost to the end of that portion of our journey. I couldn't have met Solace soon enough.

"This is pretty wild, like, when you live day to day, scrounging for food in the Outlands…" Maddy paused. "To come and see a place like this, where they have food, fucking water on tap, and licorice. It's pretty amazing to experience. If you have any form of cash in the Outlands, you can get what you need, but still at a limited supply. Here, if it's not a cash system, and I can clean up dog shit or something, to feed myself and have some shelter? Sounds like a pretty good deal to me." She surmised.

"That's what we'd like to think happens Maddy. That people like yourself can find a normal life here. Work eight hours, go home, have minimal luxuries, and enjoy your life." She smiled, looking certain she had convinced us.

"You want it like it used to be," I said.

Her face flushed, "Solace can give you more details on it." She turned to the doors. "We'll be arriving shortly."

Maddy looked over at me. "I didn't think about it like that Khadim. I wasn't around much when things were quote on quote ;'normal'". I was only a kid at the time of the war. Did people like it then?" She asked as she stared deeply into my eyes.

"People lived their lives, manifested possessions, worked endlessly, and the people in charge just kept raising the price of living. So, people had to work harder to get what they wanted. They had to pay more to get the same luxuries daily. It was empty, and repetitive. Many people never found their own happiness, relying on material things to give them snap satisfaction."

I sighed and pulled at my beard.

"Yet it was never enough for most people. Real happiness comes from within." I tapped my chest with my hand. "Just getting to do what you enjoy. Doing what it took get that, and to maintain it."Sloane watched on and added her thoughts.

"Not everyone is the same though, different people want different things."

"That's true." I agreed. "It's when you encroach on others beliefs that it becomes a problem. If you want to believe that the earth is flat, that's great. Whatever makes you happy is fine. If you were to come tell me that the earth was flat, and I told you I thought it was in fact, round. You could react in two different ways; you could give me the same respect that I gave you and just let me believe in what I want to believe. Where it didn't hurt a single person."

"Or, you could impose your beliefs on me, and insist that I needed to believe what you believed. And that if I did not, I would be against you. I must fit into your mold, or not exist anymore. I then would become motivation for you to gather others to support your cause and to push me out because of mine." I told her. "The latter was the case most of the time."

"Acceptance of others is true balance," I told Sloane.

She said nothing.

"Well fucking said." Maddy clapped her hands and nodded.

Sloane looked like she sank deep into her thoughts, after a moment she turned to me with a smile and said. "I guess I never thought about it that way before."

CHAPTER 18

SOLACE

THE DOORS OF the elevator glided open to a large room. Golden embellishments, rich ivory whites, and plush red velvet lined the lavish floors. A long hallway ran to the left and to the right. In front of us stood a set of elaborate double doors with intricate carvings of holy angels and menacing demons, on the outside of it sat a plaque with gold foil lettering in cursive that read. "Solace Serenity, Overseer of Yggdrasil."

The idea that she considered herself the Overseer, when Minh sat at the bottom with total control of the tree, seemed ignorant on her part.

"Right this way." Sloane guided us to the door. She grabbed the handles and swung the doors inwards, I watched as the blinding light spilled out of the doorway and illuminated the hallway. The overuse of light in this building confounded me. Who would want a room this bright? Turning, I saw that Maddy had put her goggles back on and chewed away at her last piece of licorice. Sloane walked in with her clipboard up to block the light some. Although half-tempted to place my goggles back on, I could not afford Jolt this upcoming information.

We stood at the entrance, Maddy and I looking forward, while Sloan hung her head to avert the light. The room smelled something like lavender, but I couldn't place the specifics of the smell, something floral.

"The Constant Khadim, and young Maddy the Power." Sloane announced us.

"Wonderful." Came a rich sultry tone from a woman with skin as dark as coal. She sat proudly behind an ivory desk. The lights began to dim a small bit, that or my eyes were adjusting. Maddy pulled out her box of cigarettes and shook the box, she was pretty calm in my opinion.

The remainder of the room appeared empty, it looked like the space went on endlessly. Just a large white desk and this woman with her rigid posture, sitting there. Seemed like a waste of good space to me.

The statuesque woman stood up and glided gracefully around the front of the desk. Her flawless charcoal skin had a thin sheen to it, and her hair was styled up into an afro. Her white pant suit, with its gold trim along the shoulders and pants, stood in stark contrast to her skin.

I smiled at her, trying to grasp how a woman could appear so beautiful in every way, aesthetically, and yet present the ugliest aura I had ever seen. Lies, murder, arson, pleasures of the flesh, torture, and much more saturated her sodden aura.

The malevolent smile that shown on her golden lips, spread wide to reveal a perfect set of teeth.

"Please, have a seat." She motioned to us with her slender fingers.

"I've got it from here." She dismissed Sloane with a flick of her wrist. Two golden leather chairs materialized in front of us. With their thick velvet cushions sporting onyx buttons all along the back, they looked like the type of chairs you'd find rich men sitting in, while they sipped upon one hundred-year-old scotch and smoked foreign cigars, prattling on about the good ol' days.

I placed my hand on the back of one of the chairs. It seemed solid enough. Maddy had already leaned back in hers when I dropped into mine.

"Cigar?" The woman offered us from an ornate box on the desk. I placed my hand up to show I wasn't interested. Maddy grabbed one all too enthusiastically, she then leaned back into her chair and placed a hand in her pocket. She produced her lighter, but Solace already held out a wavering match.

"Better flavor." Solace insisted.

Maddy leaned in and lit the cigar on the flame. Courtesy could be misleading. "So." She spread her hands out while getting to the point.

"I'm Solace." She poured herself a tall amber drink from a carafe sitting on the table. "I'm here to guide you Khadim, what questions might you have for me? I know it's been a long painstaking journey to get here."

She had no idea.

The opportunity had finally arisen for me. First thing was first.

"What the hell is a Constant?"

She grinned and nodded as if she expected this. "You've been waiting a while on that one, haven't you?" With a light clink, she set her iced tumbler on a crystal coaster.

"So, to get straight into it, you're an angel. Well, an angel of sorts anyhow."

I stared at her vacantly when she said this, *I wasn't even religious, how could I be an angel?*

She continued. "We all are really, when God and Satan walked away from this battle, God couldn't leave his beautiful world in disarray, couldn't leave his humans to pass away unnoticed. Understandably right? He had to have someone here to pass on his word and to keep the populace alive and sated. After all, we're all God's children." She opened her arms wide motioning to Maddy and I.

Maddy looked at me doubtfully with a sidelong glance over the rim of her glass.

"Why, Satan is just a fellow Constant, he just fell out of order." She focused a lot of energy into this last sentence. "See, he got a little too big for his britches and decided he knew better than God did, causing all this trouble for the humans, like Maddy here."

She walked to the front of the desk and leaned on it. "She lost her loving mother and father to demons, didn't you?" She clicked her thin tongue. "A shame, your mother was a good woman, loving and nurturing, she took good care of you. Even with that abusive father of yours.

The demons came in the night and carried your father away. Which your clever mother saw as a blessing in disguise, even though she told you otherwise."

Maddy stared daggers at Solace.

Solace picked up her glass and took a long drink, the ice clinked softly as the amber liquid journeyed into her system. She took her glasses off and sat them on the desk. Solace turned and answered Maddy's glare. I saw that she even had golden irises. The woman was truly stunning.

Maddy put her head down but continued to look Solace in the eyes. Anger flared, mixing with tears in her eyes. Maddy gripped the glass tightly in her hands. I recalled Maddy saying she watched her mother torn apart by a demon.

Solace leaned back again and relaxed, she looked satisfied she wouldn't be challenged by Maddy. "Then your mother went as well, didn't she? Torn apart from the inside out by a raging demon, right in front of you." She shook her head and tutted.

"Do you want to know why that happened?" Solace asked as Maddy tensed in her seat.

"Did you see the watch that the demon was wearing? The time piece fused to its skin? The very watch your mother bought your father for their first anniversary, before you were even a thought to them. Nothing special, but to him it was a reminder of the mistake he had made by marrying her, but also that there was something so wonderful that came out of the relationship."

Maddy sniffed and tried fighting back her emotions, tears ran down her stern gaze. Solace continued her tale.

"He gave into the lure of alcohol and hurt your mother daily, sometimes just for a negative glance she might have given him. He never could lay a hand on you though, could he? Anytime you broke something, lied, or ruined his perfect bubble? He avoided touching you and took it out on your mother. This last time he did, *he* was the demon that killed her. Did you know that Maddy?" Solace looked down her perfect nose at Maddy.

Maddy shook her head and wept. Solace continued undeterred by the emotions of my friend.

"Why would he do that, you ask? He had been taken and molded personally by the Devil to fit his own selfish needs. You are part angel after all, you were a threat to him. The very demon Satan sent wouldn't touch you because he loved you still, demon or not. So, instead he killed your loving mother, the woman he hated. Though this didn't go according to his plan, Satan was ok with this, maybe after this you would take your own life?"

She sipped from her drink.

"Satan does not cut corners to have the world for his own. He takes the worst kinds to do his deeds, your wicked father was a prime example. God emerged victorious in the battle with Satan over you though, because you survived as your father fled a second time into the darkness from your world. Unable to harm his dear Maddy."

Solace looked up at the ceiling and stretched her back like a cat.

Maddy broke down in tears. She sobbed uncontrollably next to me, her body wracked by deep breaths in between her tears. She said nothing as she sat weeping into her hands.

Solace shook her head dismissively while she looked down on Maddy. She then turned to me and offered a placid smile.

"You and Satan are cut from the same cloth Khadim. Satan was a Constant first. Why, technically you're my boss." She laughed as she grabbed the carafe filled with the amber liquor. She filled a glass with the bourbon and placed it in front of Maddy with a clunk.

She twirled her dark hand and explained, "A Constant shall arise when the balance is broken." Solace stood up and wandered around behind the desk. "This is God's word, or so the legend goes anyhow. When the Constant arrives, he will seek to right the balance that has tipped the scales." She waved her hand in a circular motion again, as if this was something she had to repeat over and over.

"In, non-biblical terms? One of us switched from good to bad. Simply put, the balance went askew." She watched as Maddy took the glass from the desk and downed it in a single gulp. Solace took the carafe over and refilled the glass for her.

Maddy clasped the glass in her shaky grip, and swallowed it down as fast as the first one.

I was worried about her.

Solace placed her glass and the carafe on the table, opened the wooden box holding the cigars, took one, clipped the end of it, and lit it for herself. She took in a deep breath and exhaled through her nostrils, thick white smoke rolled forth smelling like newly sown fields, or rich earth. She looked over at me with her golden eyes and grinned malevolently.

"You see, there are many different choirs of angels. We are the upper echelon, right before we get too..." Her eyes looked upward, searching for a word. She blew rings of smoke with the lit cigar. "Lovecraftian in our looks. Things covered in eyeballs, talking bushes, and so on. We are the people's protectors."

She shook with disgust as she spoke about the other angels.

"You, being a Constant are what people in the 4th century would've called a Dominion. Times have inevitably changed, as

many things do. You find the imbalance, like I said, then you elim-
inate it, and then finally replace it. You're the result of our folly."
She took another long drag from the cigar. She blew smoke out
between her lips towards me.

I restrained a cough.

"Here's the kicker. You, *become* the new balance. You technically get a demotion, if you will, and become a virtue like the rest
of us. Like those that you've met so far. Faul, Jolt, Avery, Terra,
Minh, and myself. That's only half of us though, we have another
six out there as well. Some of which we don't even know who they
are, but when we see them, we'll know. We each represent a different element of this world. Jolt is the storm, with power over
all things electrical, he single-handedly powers the world with
his abilities. Terra is the earth itself, he doesn't even know the full
extent to his powers, for good reason I might add. Minh is the
plant virtue, controlling any plant life he comes across, including
this very tree we are standing in, the almighty World Tree at his
whim. Avery is a mystery, we just found him thanks to you. He
was off the map, and it appears that he was trying to build a small
army of sorts, possibly to do his bidding. That's about all we could
ascertain from the humans we found at the site."

"That would make you the virtue of what?" I asked her.

"Why, I am the Virtue of serenity Khadim. I sit up here and
help humans stay peaceful. I'm the great state of calm. We all find
our way here eventually; we will go years without seeing a new
Constant. Then out of nowhere, one of you will show up, and
become one of us in due time. I have been doing this longer than
anyone almost. We've had many come and go amongst us over
the years."

I thought about this. "Like Faul and Goethe," I said aloud.

Her perfect façade cracked and her snide look faltered for a
moment. She cocked an eyebrow at the mention of the names.

"Faul, yes we knew, came in and killed the last sun Virtue

because he started to try to manipulate the sun out of its stuck position, therefore aiding Satan. He switched to his side."

She took another sip of her bourbon. "The name Goethe is one I haven't heard in many years. He fought in this war long before the current state of things. Much like you, a human who changed into a Constant. He represented what none of us were before, one of God's children. Not an angel with a burden."

"Can I ask how it is you came to know his name?" she asked me in earnest.

Apparently, she didn't have ALL the information, I thought with some satisfaction.

"So, how do Maddy and Rachel fit into this?" I asked, deflecting her question.

She changed back to the subject at hand for now, a small victory for me. "Maddy and Rachel are Powers, they're under Virtues in rank. They are information givers, whether they are aware of it or not. I'm willing to bet you know a lot about what happened just because of her."

She motioned with her chin to Maddy, who sat with her legs crossed in the chair, much calmer now. She rolled the ice around in her glass in a daze.

Maddy had explained it all to me along our journey. I hardly saw her as angelic though. Then again, the fact that I could be an angel was still almost impossible to believe.

"In fact, she's basically your guardian angel. That's mostly what Powers are, Rachel is mine," she said. "We don't own them, but they naturally gravitate towards us, I'm sure she's the reason that the two men found you in the first place."

Maddy looked up with her watery green eyes. She looked like she was in awful pain. Her eyes swam from the alcohol most likely.

"You ok?" I asked her.

She nodded with heavy lids. "It's true. I was the one who guided Reese and Anthony there. I just..." She put her hand on her chest. "I just felt, like I needed to be there by some outside force. Like, when you have a good feeling about something you know? An instinct."

I nodded at her.

"I didn't mean to get you into all this shit," she said as tears welled again in her eyes. "Bring you into this fucked up world."

I smiled at her. "My life is better with you in it Maddy. I'm happy you brought me out of that basement, we're going to fix things here." I told her with conviction.

"Actually." Solace chimed in as she stood up, placing her glass on the desk and the cigar on an ashtray.

"You are going to have to take over Faul's position. You killed him, which is unfortunate, and now you inherit his mess," Solace said as she picked up her cigar and tapped the ashes out.

"Not saying that you need to be a biker, or run a biker gang, you can do it your own way, but you do have to watch the Outlands and keep his... excuse me, your territory." She picked up a cigar cutter and sliced her remaining cigar after the ashes.

The audacity of this woman.

"That doesn't sound like what I planned on doing. Why would you suggest that?" I asked her.

"You'll assume his role as Virtue and that's that. If it doesn't fix the balance, you'll have another Constant that shows up to challenge whomever it is that's out of balance. That's how it works." She gave a dismissive smile and put the cigar back into the box.

"No. That's what you would *like*. Not what's going to happen." I grinned at her.

I laughed this time. I laughed so hard that my stomach ached. I slapped my leg as my laughter echoed through the room, and most likely, back down the hallway, and across the opening outside to those within Yggdrasil. I watched as Maddy laughed quietly and then sat with a grin on her face. Solace stood, her brow deeply furrowed, and her golden irises piercing deep into mine. She didn't laugh. She didn't smile. I watched as her façade shattered.

"Looks like you're not *always* the picture of calm." Maddy snickered.

It was my turn to let her know what I thought about all of this.

"I don't do well with people telling me what I have to do. If I didn't want to come here, even though I had everyone telling me that I *had* to come here, I would've walked away. It's my nature. I have my own balance to attend to, not God or the Devil's agenda. Fuck them."

I shook my head and sat up in my seat.

"You've got his powers though, the powers of the sun." She pointed at my hands. "We saw you burn that door hinge off, and make the windows for the car!"

I groaned as I held the goggles up in my hand.

"It's these isn't it." I pulled the goggles off from around my neck. "Jolt modified them and you guys can see out of them 24/7 huh?"

I couldn't believe that I trusted what Jolt said.

"It's disgusting that you guys watch so much. Fucking voyeurs. You're not God, you're a perverted version of him, people deserve their privacy." I stood up from my seat.

I thought about the hillock of shit I'd dealt with in those past few days. She was an idiot for trying to tell me I had to fall under order of what some legend said. I was done with her bullshit.

"Sorry Patty."

I melted the goggles in my hand, the molten metal began to run down my hands and onto the floor, the small plastic bits burst into flames, an acrid smell filled the room as it burned. The goggles transformed into a thing of the past, just like their ideology was about to.

CHAPTER 19
TRUE COLORS

"KHADIM, KHADIM, KHADIM" I heard from the other side of the room as I turned to see Jolt promenading towards us. Each step he took was with care, as if to add drama to his entrance. He spread his arms wide and looked at us with his sunglasses-covered face.

"You think that you're the first one to show up thinking you can control us? That you aren't going to fall in line with what is preordained by GOD HIMSELF?!" He laughed loudly and placed his arms across his chest. "You're just another fool. Humans can be so arrogant."

He leaned over and pointed his index finger at me. "You're better than God, Khadim? No. You are ignorant, more so than I could have ever imagined." Another Jolt walked over from the other side of the room, an exact replica of this one. "We are Legion Khadim, you will follow the rules in place, or you will perish for it." The duo laughed in stereo this time.

I'd been chased down by a towering demon earlier today, the idea that a pair of robots might frighten me was entertaining. The fact that I could even think that with a straight face should have showed him how far I'd come. I stayed in my seat while Solace watched the Jolts, she eventually went and sat back in her chair, seemingly comfortable she might be safe.

"Look, I don't want this getting ugly," Solace said with a genuine smile. It would have almost been warm, if it wasn't for her frosty demeanor. Crossing her long legs and smoothing out her silk skirt, she seemed like her calm self once the Jolt twins had intervened. "You already killed Faul, whether that was what you were awakened for or not. It isn't really up to me, it was preordained. However, if we allow you to kill anyone else, it will offset the balance even further." She explained to me.

"Seems like it might fix a few problems if you ask me," I told her.

"Not really," she said. "You see, God is infallible, which means that his rules cannot be broken. He knows and decides all, he's never made a mistake in his existence, and even Satan's fall was preordained." "Having free will is for the humans, *you* have to do what is outlined in the holy word. Not the Bible, but the word from Him!" She pointed up.

I thought about that as she said it.

"That's funny, he's never once spoken to me," I told her. "One day I'm strapped to a gurney being used as a human pincushion, and the next I'm supposed to be some sort of holy avenger for a God I don't even follow? I didn't believe in him until I woke up anyhow! Not to mention, I *am* human, so I have a right to free will."

Kind of hard to downplay the shape of the world without believing that "God" did it. While we talked, the two Jolts merged into one, I watched as they blurred together into a single figure. He dropped a few ice cubes into a liquor glass and swirled it around. Those robots were the real deal, they could even drink and probably eat. If I couldn't see auras, I'd have had a hard time differentiating between the real and the fake Jolts.

"The best part of all this is what happens if I don't follow what you want? What if I continue to play it my way and don't become a virtue?"

Solace's grin soured yet again when I said this, that calm of hers waned by the second.

"There are twelve of us Khadim, thirteen including you. Six for God, six for the Devil. Balanced. When you don't fall in line, that leaves us at an imbalance. You killed Faul, knocking our number to eleven, you take his place, and we become twelve again. " She sat up in her chair and placed her elbows on her legs.

"Right now, we're at an impasse since you haven't stepped down to take his place. You must do this willingly for it to work though. If you do not, and you never accept it? We can't have another Constant to fix future imbalances. The system gets thrown off, don't you see that?" She raised her hands up in exasperation.

"You are God's will, sent here to create balance. If it doesn't balance out, God can't send another one, because that would mean that God was wrong! If he's wrong, the world winks out of existence!" She snapped her fingers.

"You're it. YOU ARE HIS WILL. So, the balance will stay off, but it stays off because you're not assuming the role given to you! Which is why, in situations like this." She put her head down and stretched, looking over at Jolt.

"We usually kill the Constant and reset the balance ourselves. So, you must see, that you need to willingly take over the role given to you, for your own good."

She spoke with anger filled tears in her eyes, while Jolt just stood there and sipped his bourbon. I watched as he smiled behind the glass. It made me reach into my pocket and feel for Goethe's dagger. It sat in the inside pocket of my jacket, against my heart.

"Seems to me like you guys are the one fucking with God's system if you've had to do this before," I said. "Maybe you don't understand his will after all?"

Jolt leaned in over the table, the rich bourbon smell permeating from his mouth. He whispered into my ear. "You need to be more, *malleable* Constant."

"Maurelius," I said under my breath, the man in black from the dream still fresh in my mind from Avery's Deep Diner.

He grinned so wide, it was as if his face had split in two.

"Heh." He started, "Heh heh. Hahaha HAHAHA HAHAHAHAHA." He launched into a torrent of laughter. Throwing his body back and his arms out, his body quaked. He wiped tears from his eyes when he turned and spoke to Solace.

"Solace, this is what I'm here for! To keep this line fresh." He motioned with his hands at me. "Fools like this appear once every few hundred years and try to make this world…" he lifted his voice several octaves to mock me. "A better place for the huumanns." He sloshed his drink in the glass while making wide gestures. "Why should this human be any different?!"

"I recall seeing you in your dream Constant. Fun fact, you know that by controlling electricity, I can jump right into your dreams through your brain. Science is fucking great man!" He took off his glasses and his yellow eyes flickered brightly. Strands of his hair came loose from his pompadour and dangled over his face in disarray.

"That dream about Goethe was a message. A WARNING." He shouted with his arms out wide. "I tried to help you not make a stupid decision about this!" He slammed his tumbler on the table. It shattered across the wood. Glass plunged to the floor. Blood dripped down his hand. He swiped it across his face leaving a red smear. "Guess it didn't work." He cackled like a lunatic.

Maddy shot up in her seat and grabbed for the machete she kept strapped to her leg.

Solace reacted quickly and turned to her with an arm out.

"Be at peace," Solace said to her as Maddy slumped over in her chair and then onto the floor.

She turned to me. "Can't go wasting good powers," Solace said as she lit up her cigar again.

"I'm not going to kill you yet Constant," Jolt said, shaking his head, his hair bobbing back and forth.

"I'm going to show you what you've missed. History will guide you." He reached for my head with his bloody hands.

I was done with his nonsense.

I grabbed the knife from my pocket and buried it deep into Jolt's forehead. There was a brief pause, he went cross eyed, staring at it in his forehead. "Hoowwww..." He trailed off as I pulled it free. Red ichor spewed out onto the desk and all over my hand and forearm. Even if it was just a robot, it felt fantastic stabbing that asshole. I still hadn't seen the real Jolt since the desert. I would find him though, that was for damn sure.

"Where are you?' I asked out loud. "You're a fucking coward."

"I'll have my people contact yours, don't worry Constant." I heard from all around me. Solace shot up out of her seat. I guessed she lost control over Maddy because she also sprang from the floor again and produced her machete before I could react. Maddy leapt over the table and chopped the machete straight down onto Solace's left shoulder. Blood splattered across Maddy's face.

"Bitch," Solace screamed. Crimson blood oozed down her jacket, the red stood in a stark contrast to the white room. As blood splashed onto her desk where Solace had served us bourbon and cigars, she grabbed her shoulder and broke the blade in half with a halfhearted slap. She lifted her left leg and kicked Maddy in gut, sending her flying back across the room in a heap.

Solace hovered above the ground and began to shimmer. I charged at her and drove the dagger deep into her thigh. She fell to the floor, grabbing at herself. I could smell her leg smoking. When I removed the dagger, blood congealed at the surface, and the wound cauterized instantaneously. A mechanism of the blade that I had not foreseen.

Solace shoved her arms forward with her hand in a palm out position. The desk flew forward and slammed into my chest. The air escaped my lungs, and the pressure threatened to incapacitate me. I slid back under the immense weight of the desk. Several of my ribs cracked under the pressure. My chest was on fire.

"Why is it so hard to get you human Constants to accept His will?" she shouted as she stood up. "Why even use humans?! They're all so jaded. Free will is bullshit." She threw her hands forward again and propelled the desk back further into me.

It pushed me along the floor past the front doors to the hallway. I grappled for carpet, walls, anything that could slow me down, but I just couldn't get a hold of anything. The doors slammed open into the hallway, revealing a small balcony. We were balanced upon the twelve hundredth and ninety ninth floor complete with an impossible fall to my death beyond.

I tried shoving the desk off my chest as hard as I could, a futile effort as my strength waned from the struggle. Solace limped towards me with her hand out and I began to think about how awful this situation had become, how if I died, Maddy would go back to a world that used her, and would eventually leave her a withered husk. I thought about how the humans in in that world had no clue about the corruption at the top...

"AAAAAHHHHHH" I shouted at the top of my lungs as I placed all my strength into shoving the desk of off me.

A blast of pressure powered through my chest and arms. The desk exploded into flames. In one glorious moment, all that hulking weight upon my chest, dissipated. Ashes kicked up from its remains, and swirled in the air.

The ground smoldered and smoked, turned moist again as water rained down from above. The building protected itself from the fire. The sudden flow of liquid quickly turned to steam.

I stood up. My body had become engulfed by flames. I had changed. My arms became wringed in flames, my chest a burning beacon, and I watched as more flames ran up and across my entire body, not harming me in any way. I felt powerful, I had become one with the fire. The water that fell from the ceiling did nothing to the flames that flickered around me. My dagger morphed into a long flaming spear. It scraped the ground as I moved it about in the air, the velvet carpet turned black in my wake. The tip sprouted three flaming prongs, like a burning trident. It must have been Goethe's spear. I was his legacy and I would bring the balance to humanity.

A chair sailed through the air and crashed into my chest. It slammed me into the metal elevator door. The chair burned to ashes as it fell over the edge into the chasm of Yggdrasil.

The doors bowed inward as I landed, and broke my possible fall into the shaft. I leaned forward on the door and ran full force towards the now hovering Solace. She too, had taken on another form, a source of pure light. Her body undulated a white glow. Her lean silhouette was the only thing that gave reason to her form. I didn't care what she looked like, that bitch was going down.

I charged forth and drove at her with my spear. She rolled out of the way. The second chair crashed me into the wall in front of the office. She smashed my leg with that last shot. My shin splintered under the pressure of the attack. My body ached, and it infuriated me even more. The flames on my body flickered between blue and orange. This woman represented everything I hated.

My body glided upwards, the powers fully manifesting within my body. My wounded leg knitted together as we stared each other down.

"You really want to die instead of taking over Faul's role? It's that simple," she shouted at me as her form wavered, her body a glowing, blinding white light. I didn't answer her.

I charged, swinging my trident again at her. She maneuvered around each strike like a practiced cobra dodging attacks. Solace leaned back beneath a swipe, and spun in the air bringing down her booted foot on the top of my head. Blinding pain overwhelmed my senses. I staggered a moment, taking in a deep breath, then returned the blow by bringing my leg up in turn. The heel of my right foot buried itself in her left hip. She spun back through the air out of control.

I had underestimated my strength in this form, and watched as she crashed through the wall and into another room beyond it.

The hole in the wall glowed brightly, the ashes of destruction still burned from the flames. The room flickered as lights were smashed from Solace crashing through it. Water still fell from the ceiling making a constant swell of steam in the area. When I peered inside of it to find her, she struck me with both hands clasped together in a hammer fist onto my shoulder. I fell onto the ledge of the hole, the wall collapsing underneath me and choking the area with dust.

I didn't have much time to react as Solace punted me into the railing across the hallway. Her strength, equal to mine. I flew through the dust choked air, crashing hard into the steel barrier between myself and the insane drop. The bar bent outward and my back snapped uncomfortably.

She continued her assault, and bellowed madly as she tried to drop her knee down into my chest. I rolled towards her and swung up with the trident, catching her and flipping her into the ceiling. A loud metallic clang rang out as she bashed the back of her skull into the metal pipes above her, it was a strong shot. The tiles crashed down around her and onto the floor. Blood ran down her still undulating body. She looked dazed. This was my chance. I put all my anger into a deafening cry and hurled the spear through the air at her. The spear plunged deep into her side and into the floor. She wailed in agony. Her silhouette on the left side erupted. The wall and floors behind her doused in gobs of smoldering gore.

She flickered back and forth, before looking down and running her hands through the thick sludge of ooze leaking from her side. She dropped to the ground and clutched at her side. Her body blinked and returned to its original form.

I watched as she flashed brightly. Each time she closed her eyes to return to her improved form, but for some reason it wouldn't work. She wept as she realized she was trapped in her human form, how fitting. She grinned at me with blood on her perfect teeth. It amused me greatly. "All the weakness of a human. Yet, none of the empathy and understanding that it's ok to be yourself. Without having to control what others think." I placed a boot on her chest and pulled my trident from her side, it sloshed loudly from the wound. She bled out onto the floor, lying on the ground and stared up at me with thick viscous fluid running from her mouth and head. This time the wounds did not seal from the weapon.

"What happens when I kill you?" I asked her.

"The next Constant will take over my role." She spit a mouth full blood onto the dust covered floor. "The powers go back into the pool until they show up." She grimaced as she gripped her side in anguish, her face twisted up into a painful mask of blood and tears. "Why couldn't you just go with the laws?"

I relished in her pain. Knowing that I stopped someone like Solace felt right, one step closer to my peace. To think she helped Terra, there had to be more to it.

"I'm human, I guess it's in my nature to question things. I don't know how someone like you ever had it in your heart to rescue Terra without having your own endgame in mind." I grimaced at her.

"Terra is just as big of a fool as you are, he doesn't even know half of what he's capable of! When I die, he will never find out either!" More blood ran down her face and neck. "Jolt will end you, mark my words."

I laughed at her.

"Jolt may be my end when this all comes to a head, but it won't be to avenge you. You think he is on your side? Jolt played you. You were just a tool for him to manipulate, you never had any power, he was the one behind the scenes. I thought this would have been apparent to you. He never gave two shits about you. Don't kid yourself." I placed the point of my weapon above her collarbone. She closed her eyes and tears ran down her face.

This conversation was over.

I plunged the trident deep into her throat, watching the prongs bury themselves to the crossbar. "I am my own person," I said, as I tore it out and watched as her eyes went vacant and her body went still.She smoldered and smoked on the floor. The corpse vibrated violently back and forth. A blinding flash cut throughout the air. I blinked my eyes. The light subsided, and Solace was no more.

This time, after I had killed a virtue, I felt nothing. I didn't feel happiness, sadness, anger, or anything of the sort. My body didn't become younger; my powers didn't get any stronger. A moment in time that passed without notice.

I finally knew what I was now, and what people told me I was supposed to do, but this was not the path I was going to take. I was still my own person.

CHAPTER 20
UNDER NEW MANAGEMENT

I RETURNED TO Maddy and found her unconscious body splayed out on the floor. Dried blood clung to the corner of her mouth. Shaking her shoulder, I tried to wake her up.

"Maddy, it's time to go," I said to her.

She groaned and proceeded to vomit the bourbon up on the floor. She had a coughing fit for a minute, and her voice shook as she looked up at me.

"Fuck that. This place has to go," she rasped.

"What do you mean? These people didn't do anything." I gestured to Yggdrasil. "This whole thing is a palace for the powerful to reign over the weak minded. Those cities out there are just traps for people to show up in and die! Like a fucking roach motel! They check in, but never check out!" Maddy sat up and explained.

I thought about what Jolt said, and how they were all sheep that needed to be herded. Maddy was right. We had to turn the electricity off, people would have to figure real life out on their own, not be force fed mind numbing nonsense. They would have to be weaned in order to grow. Yggdrasil stood as a symbol of times past. God's power over others and Satan's descent into hell to manipulate the world. The whole damned balance needed a reset, this whole Constant thing maybe had some merit after all. I wondered if I hadn't just found my path thanks to Maddy.

"My guardian angel," I said to her.

"Fuck you," she said through a laugh.

I picked her up, my ribs aching as I lifted her. The healing process went slowly now that I wasn't in my other form.

"Jolt controls the power Maddy. If we're going to turn it off permanently, he must die." I explained.

"That's all well and good, but to kill him, we need to find him, and neither you nor I have the time or energy to do that right now." She said to me through a grunt of pain.

I considered where we were though and what could be done. "I do have an idea though. This place has to have a loudspeaker, something to communicate to everyone at once." I said to her.

We walked back into the room and found the room dark now. Monitors lined the walls and lit the room up with a light glow. I scanned through them as fast I could. I saw sections on the wall that read Saint Anthony, Saint Sandoval, etc. The keyboard had been divided up into each subdivision of the cities outside. There to the right, a wall of monitors showed every floor in the building, many small screens in the field of large screens. The only place that didn't have cameras was the Outlands. It may have been the safest place after all.

A small microphone sat on the counter, I walked over to it and tested the buttons. Different lights and panels lit up when I pressed them. It seemed to be interconnected to a lot of different things, judging by the panel, most lights were on mainly in the Saint Sandoval section right now.

On the side, next to the switch, there was a button that said Rachel on it. *How convenient.* The light flickered black and white. I pressed the button down and said, "Rachel."

I released the button and waited. "Yes, this is Rachel." She answered and I finally knew who she was talking to all those times. "Khadim?" she asked, surprise resonating in her voice.

"Yes, I need your help. Where is Terra?" I asked her.

"He's here with me. We're both at the garage in Saint Sandoval. They're fixing the vehicles for us," she told me. "Khadim?" she asked with concern in her voice.

"Yeah?" I answered her.

"You killed her didn't you?" She asked me bluntly, and without waiting for me to answer, she continued. "I can't feel her anymore; she was always there. I couldn't get away from it. That connection is gone now. It's like there is a void in my head."

"Yes, Solace is gone," I replied.

"I only worked with you for a little while, but seeing what you have in mind for this world, just know I'm with you," she said. "Nice to have that voice out of my head now, I feel in control again."

This made me wonder if Maddy felt like that with me. If what Solace said about Powers was true, she was inherently drawn to me, which gave me some sort of control over her. I hated that.

"You and Terra need to get those cars and come to Yggdrasil to get us. You'll have to get here soon, be quick."

Rachel replied, "We'll be there as fast as we can."

I depressed the button.

"What are you doing?" Maddy asked and then her eyes lit up. "We're going to knock this place down aren't we?" she said in her excited voice all too loudly.

Each monitor flickered on at the same time, with the same face on it. Jolt.

"I can't help but feel you're judging me Constant." He smiled wide. "Please, from now on, let us not pretend. My name is Maurelius, I am the longest living Virtue.

Solace was merely another tool for me to manipulate, she so easily followed everything I said to her without question. She wanted power, so I gave her the illusion power. She wanted to be in charge, so I placed her at the head of the world's largest structure. She felt like she ruled those people. It was I who owned her, every step of the way. This world is at my will. I know the system, and where God fucked up. I've found that loophole that prevents him from interfering with me. That is except for the Constants.

I've killed hundreds of your kind over the years, and you won't be my last one Khadim. Even if you are proving to be a bit more resilient than most," he said.

"I want you to know, I know what you are about to do. That building is the finest piece of architecture and technology to ever grace our shitstain of a world. If you destroy it, thousands will die at your hands. Can you live with that on your conscience?" He removed his glasses and his eyes glowed brightly.

"These people made their choices, they wanted to put themselves into this position." I pointed at the monitors around me.

"They wanted to be above the others. The rest of the masses outside in Ouroboros wanted to dull their senses by zoning out to your televisions, to your shows. You've already killed these people Maurelius. They just don't know it yet. Those that choose to wake up and live will be able to make their own decisions from now on. I'll give them a warning like you gave me. It will be up to them to decide."

"I won't let you do this." The monitors shut off abruptly.

Sloane appeared from the other room with the power cable in her hand.

"All that power, and she still used wall plugs," she chuckled. Too bad this building was built when it was." "I'm tired of this place, I want out." she said without trepidation. "I've served these people for long enough and I want to live my own life. I believe in what you said."

I smiled. Glad to see some people were taking to the idea.

"How do we get a message out to everyone?" I asked her.

"Use the microphone, flip that blue switch there. It's the intercom. It will reach everyone within the walls that is near a monitor, which should be just about everyone, and don't worry about Jolt. We have our own network here, and his only way in just got unplugged."

He didn't have power from afar for the moment.

I flipped the switch and I sent out a message to the public at large.

CHAPTER 21
THE WARNING

AT THE SANCTUARY gas station in Saint Sandoval the store clerk watched as every monitor in the store flickered to life. A family in Saint Andrews enjoying "Get the Dollar!" watched the screen on their television turn to snow.

Anthony Smith played on his computer, living in a simulated world where he could be an orc or a goblins when his screen flickered off and on.

A baseball game in Saint Christopher's was put on hold because the infield screen, which advertised Rhapsody Cola flipped to a man with tan skin, a mane of black hair, and a month old beard. He had the coldest aqua eyes, and his stare made everyone pay attention. He was dirty and sported various black marks on his face from a possible altercation.

Who was this man?

Where was Solace? Everyone wondered as the man spoke.

"Hello, my name is Khadim Gray. I have killed your Overseer, Solace; she is no longer in control of your lives. I am unable to locate a man named Maurelius, known to you as Johnny Jolt. These people seek to control your lives with television, monotony, day jobs, and video games. Maurelius told me you people are sheep, and that we the angels are here to be your shepherds."

The man ran his hand through his beard. His face was tired, and haggard. He seemed unhappy he had to give this message to everyone. "I am going to set you all free, though it will not be easy. You will have to fight for yourself, follow your own paths, and provide for yourselves and your families. You do not need our control to have a happy life, make your own purpose. Leave each other to your own devices and accept one another for what you all are, humans. This is impossible in your current state of hibernation, idly clinging to your electronic sedation."

He let out a heavy breath full of sadness.

"I am going to open every gateway out. This city was built on lies, a foundation of empty promises. You rot in here, just as the fruit that falls from the World Tree does, waiting to be burned away by those above you. You have twenty-four hours to vacate. After that this existence, you know and cling to, will be your end. This is your one and only warning. Do not take this lightly, it is time to reset the balance."

The television screens went black. The stream of media went silent, never to turn on again. And the city of Ouroboros fell into pandemonium.

CHAPTER 22
THE SEPARATION OF EARTH AND SUN

KHADIM TURNED TO see Minh walking in the room.

"Balance is to be restored my friend?" he asked.

I nodded and grinned at him. I then took his hands in mine and told him.

"I need you to destroy the building Minh. Shake the tree free of the infection." He shook his head in acknowledgment. "I already know what must be done."

He let go of my hands and bowed graciously.

"The tree is due to be purged. It will take time, and it will be devastating to the cities in the tree's shadow. With your warning, many lives will be saved." He nodded and creased his brows. "And those that do not heed it, will go the way of Sodom and Gomorrah."

With the plan in place, I left to find Terra and Rachel at the bottom of the building. I instructed Minh to let them inside.

"This is crazy Khadim!" Terra stomped through the opening, his muscles taut with anger. "People are fleeing the city in droves, driving out to the land of demons!" He shook his head in disapproval. "They'll get torn apart!" He shouted at me and motioned towards the outside.

I stopped him and explained.

"The balance of the world is already shifting. Once they get past the demons, they can begin to resettle on their own accord. They can harvest their own crops, make their own territories, and claim their own land. Not having to pay for it to someone who doesn't own it in the first place. Surviving won't be an easy task. But, it will make for a stronger world. If God wants to help, I invite him to do so. I control no one, I seek only to break down the control that these others have. Jolt is next to fall."

Terra shook his head and gave me an intense stare. Rachel listened quietly with her arms crossed. She walked over to me and looked me in the eyes.

"I'm with you." Rachel said with a clenched fist.

Terra shook his head back and forth and looked wide-eyed at Rachel next.

"You too?!" He snapped at her.

She turned and addressed Terra. "He's right. These people have no free will in their current state! They're locked into the televisions and if we just leave this place here, Jolt will just find a way to turn the power back on. This place controls all of the Dark's power! It has to be done." She turned and walked in past me to the entrance. She waited by the elevator.

Terra watched her go and wiped angry tears from his face. He turned to me, his eyes, red and moist.

"I can't support you in this, man. There are going to be too many innocent people who lose their lives." He shouted and hit the wall, cracking the concrete open. "Just because they're stupid or stubborn doesn't mean they need to die!"

"I agree with you," I said. "Which is why I gave the warning, those who stay behind are committed to this world, run by people who seek to control them. That's their choice."

"Aren't you doing that too?" Terra said. "You're telling them that they have to leave, or die."

I shook my head.

"I didn't tell them they had to leave, I gave them that choice. I told them that the world was going to fall upon them if they didn't wake up." I looked him in his hazel eyes. "The decision is up to them. I can't give any more time than that, you know Jolt will find a way in. These people need this chance at freedom. If I knock out this structure, the power here is gone. No more control for Jolt. Should I leave them to his devices? I'm giving them the option to find their own path. They're wasting away here." Terra shook his head once more. He stood with tears in his eyes. "No, they need freedom, there has to be another way though." he said again.

"What other way? Wait and fight Jolt here? He has a legion of those duplicates he could send in at any point. What am I going to do against that here? I'm offering these people a way out. The building falls and these people are free, the tree is free, and balance can be restored here."

Terra looked at me with sympathy in his eyes. His eyes were stern but understanding. "I cannot be a part of this.""Terra, if you don't want to stand with me, or support the idea. Its ok, you can leave too. This place is going to reset in about seventeen hours with or without you here," I told him.

"Why did you kill Solace?" he asked. "What did she do that was so bad you had to kill her? She saved me!"

"She and Jolt were going to kill me if I wouldn't fall into their box. Terra, I'm not the first human Constant who wanted to be left alone. With structures like this, and the powers of virtues, humans can never live free," I said.

"If I can single handedly prevent new Constants from coming to this world, I can do something good for humanity. I can stop others from having these powers. I can stop other virtues from corrupting society to mold itself to their will. I will find the other virtues who do this, and end them!"

Terra's conviction on the matter never wavered.

I patted my chest. "Don't you see? I can stop this system put in place by the highest powers! I can staunch the bleeding! Faul and Solace are gone! We're down to ten people who could control humanity. Powers have no influence on humans, only what is ordained by God and Satan. I'm my own man amongst angels and demons." Tears rolled down Terra's cheeks. "I can't," he said. "I won't stop you, but someone has to be able to keep you in check should you become too obsessed with this."

"She lied to you Terra," I said to him. "Solace hid the truth from you, and took what she knew to her grave. Only Jolt knows what you're capable of now. He controlled her, all of this. He's the great manipulator. Don't be naïve. Find your own way, and we'll cross paths again."

He listened and seemed to consider what I said, then without another word. Terra turned around and drifted back to Pearl. Minh and I watched him go.

Turning, I headed back up the elevator.

I walked out of the elevator to see Maddy sitting on the floor smoking the cigar that she had gotten from Solace. She saw Rachel and gave her a nod to acknowledge her. Rachel laughed and shook her head.

"Still alive huh?" Rachel asked.

"Don't sound so disappointed," Maddy said, blowing a long line of smoke out of her mouth.

There at the top of the Yggdrasil, I looked over the balcony, truly a breathtaking site. Five miles up and all the world to see in front of us. The building had turned into a beehive. People of all shapes and sizes fled en masse out of the building.

Cars and trucks poured out for hours. The gas stations ran dry for some people, forcing them to find another manner of transportation. People helped other people leave. At the same time, I saw rioting in the streets and homes being broken into. No one would miss those types. Without any limits on territory, people flooded towards Yggdrasil, crisscrossing all of those who fled in the dark. A whole new world at their disposal, perhaps there would be shelter here in the aftermath. People could salvage the waste to make a new home for themselves. Though it seemed counterproductive to me. Like rebuilding a house in a swamp that kept swallowing your home.

Maddy walked over and placed an arm around my shoulder. Touch was something I had almost forgotten about, it came at a good time for me. Nice to have friends again.

"Terra bailed huh?" she asked through smoke choked breaths.

"Yes, he said I was the one being controlling," I told her.

She looked at me incredulously and launched into a very Maddy sequence.

"You're just changing the paths available to people. You have woken up a world of sleeping people and set a fire under their asses. You are telling people-" She turned with her arms open. "Make your own fucking life. Stop relying on others and go be you." She put the cigar back in her mouth and fumed.

"I should've just had you do the announcement," I said.

"Fuck that, I would've been telling 'em to get the fuck out!" She smiled. "Way less eloquent than that shit you said all ominous and mysterious like."

"Mass hysteria should come with a bit of refinement, and a sprinkle of doubt," she said, pinching her fingers tightly in front of her face.

"Sorry about Terra though," she said. "He'll come around, even if it doesn't seem like it right now. He's a good guy with a solid moral compass."

"He told me he was going to be the one who keeps me in balance," I said with sadness in my voice.

"Good! Then you have someone to always watch out that you don't become what you hate." She puffed away on the cigar. It smelled fantastic, like fresh fields.

As usual, she provided a good point.

Sloane walked overholding a flipchart in her hands with many different pages. The top of which said, *Top Secret*. Such a cliché, who the hell labeled things that were Top Secret, with a gigantic stamp that said, Top Secret? What store produced those stamps? I hoped it would get crushed when the place went down.

"This is the list of all the people we know who are virtues," said Sloane. "This also includes a list of known Powers who are attached to each virtue."

"Good information to have," I said, taking the clipboard. "I'll look it over."

She nodded.

I spent several hours pouring over the details. I read that each virtue had an opposite. Which means that Maurelius actually has an opposite in Terra, which is why he would want keep his potential limited. My sun, had an unnamed moon. Death was out there for Life. This would prove interesting, an unfallen virtue in that role. I would need to find some way to find each of these people, and possibly end them, or befriend them.

Sloane said we could take the documents she'd gathered, with us. She hated to waste information. She also let me know that there were also endless amounts of logs detailing the humans who lived within the city walls.

"Keep the information on the virtues, but burn the human information, no more control."

She looked at me with her sapphire eyes and nodded. I expected some sort of protest, but she gave none.

The time came up quickly, and there was something I still wanted to know.

CHAPTER 23

TREADING THE THIRTEENTH FLOOR

I WALKED TO the elevator and looked for a thirteen hundred button. Much to my dismay I didn't see one, but I did remember there was an urban legend that people didn't believe in having a thirteenth-floor due to the number thirteen being an unlucky number.

So, I scanned back through and did end up locating a fourteen hundred. I found it in the menu button, a golden button amongst the white ones. I pressed it, and the doors closed shut. The broken door dangled on the inside a little bit. You could still see my back imprint in it. That was a close scrape with a huge fall.

The bell dinged and the doors swooshed open.

The room in front of me featured a wall of impenetrable jet black, impossible to see through. I stepped inside.

I heard footsteps stomping towards me. I stood my ground near to the elevator in case I had to make a quick escape. A black silhouette in the darkness appeared. Dressed in golden armor, he wore a beautiful golden mask that reflected the small amount of light from the open elevator doors. I knew this man. This was Goethe.

I thought he'd died. He was impaled by Maurelius's plowshare in my dream. Yet, he stood there in front of me, and took his helmet off. His scarred face was a mess, but his armor glimmered pristine and polished. "I hope the weapon came in handy," he said in a gravely baritone voice. "I kind of cheated the system to get it to you. Maurelius can make dreams, but I can manifest within them, as well. It is God's way of balancing Maurelius's powers."

I stood amazed at this and nodded in acknowledgement.

"What is this place?" I asked him in bewilderment.

"Purgatory, the only place we can't escape," he said as many other figures joined at his side. "When you're a human that turns into a Constant, your soul is bonded with God. He owns it, and you cannot get it back unless you complete his will. It has something to do with that whole, being infallible bit. Each of us here are previous human Constants. Not one of us has ever made the progress you have. I sent that dream about Maurelius to let you know the dangers you will find."

The crowd behind him murmured.

I thought about that, Maurelius said it was him who gave me the dream, and here was Goethe saying the same thing. Both believed they were in control of it.

I looked at the many different people in the room, they came from all walks of life. Every race, sexuality, and personality represented. The thought of so many failures almost overwhelmed me.

"How do I stand a chance when you all failed doing what I'm doing now?" I asked him flatly.

"You have a tenacity none of us have had, you won't back down. Even when a human Constant decides to take the place of a fallen virtue, he is still human in nature. Therefore, he failed in his task of bringing balance.

We believe the only way to fix all this, is to wipe out the virtues and reset the balance entirely. What you're doing now is on so much of a smaller scale. It's the foundation for overcoming Maurelius and the others."

"That means the good must go too?" I asked as the realization hit me.

"Though it seems unfair, no matter the side it starts on, each wave causes the world to quake," he said.

"I understand." I nodded to him.

It had to be my way though, I thought.

"Keep the blade, it will be your weapon to combat evil, it served me well." He grabbed my blade from my jacket pocket. He began to stretch it and mold it into a longer blade. It glowed like molten metal as he shaped it into a short sword. The scabbard a bright orange that stood out from the black outfit from the biker I found. He handed it pommel first, back to me.

"This will be a bit more practical, if you think of it as a spear when you transform into the sun, it will change as well." He smiled. "This is the weapon bestowed to us by God, it negates the virtues powers. If you use it on a virtue who can control water, he will no longer be able to control the water. Just as Solace could no longer use her powers. It shuts them off. If you remove it, the effect minimizes depending upon the damage done to them with the blade."

"Maurelius is the great deceiver, always keep your guard up Khadim," he said. "The blade will only be able to stop the powers of the real embodiment of him." He grimaced. "If you ever do kill Maurelius without using the blade, if any electricity is left remaining anywhere nearby, he can resurface. You must kill him with the blade to end him forever."

He pointed at the holy sword.

"Your time is up Constant. You must go now; this will be the last time we meet in person until the next life." He placed his fist across his chest in a sign of respect and bowed his head to me. One by one, the rest of the Constants faded away. I turned back and stepped into the elevator, and headed down to get everyone else.

I stepped forward out of the elevator and found my friends waiting. Maddy, Sloane, Rachel, and Minh walked into the elevator to join me. I pushed the button and we began our descent.

The elevator walls turned into a clear glass as they had before on the original ascent. The trek down showed that much of the population had successfully left. I did however see a small handful of people milling around the various floors. The warning was there, and the destruction needed to be done. They had made their choice.

We reached the bottom floor and disembarked. Minh opened the tree limbs, allowing us an easy passage to walk through. The rest headed to the van while Minh and I stayed behind.

I looked at him and he smiled. "We wanted this for so long Khadim. I knew that you would be the one to accomplish it after the trees whispered to me about you." He placed his hands on the tree and rubbed it like one might pet an animal he loved.

"This is for the greater good, the tree has been in pain since they built this structure onto it. You know it was Jolt who ordered it? He said we could use the tree to make a new life for ourselves with the humans doing our work. I felt pain every time they placed a beam into the tree, each one a dagger into my soul. I could feel what the tree felt when they broke branches to make way for each new floor. This is the tree connecting Heaven and Hell together. This purgatory they built to house those who were already dying."

gTears wet Minh's face. "I am ready to shake the dead leaves from the tree." He looked up with his soulful eyes lovingly at branches and roots protruding from the wall. He placed an empathetic hand on a root that came from the wall.

I gave him a long hug. He smiled at me and wiped his eyes. "Don't worry, the plants will take care of me. I have no fear."

I turned and hurried to the van.

CHAPTER 24
YGGDRASIL RETURNS

MADDY SAT IN the driver seat and I jumped in on the passenger side, finally consenting to her driving.

"He's not coming?" Maddy asked, looking at Minh waving at us in the distance.

"No. He knows what he has to do," I said as he turned and roots came up to block the outside entrance. It had already begun.

"Hope so," she said. "Buckle up! Are you trying to get yourself killed?"

Maddy turned the van around and drove away as fast we could. I watched the clock on the dashboard tick down minute after minute. We had a little less than two hours to get to the outskirts. Minh said that it would take him a few hours to shatter the foundation. The building wouldn't topple until that was completed. He said that he would never forget this day, that I was humanity's only hope for balance.

The ground began to rumble and we passed the first gate out.

The scene in the dark proved to be gruesome. Freshly overturned cars littered the freeway. We used the middle lane for expediency, having an advantage others did not. People were still making their way out, leaving later than they should have. I watched as buildings in the distance burned, many neighborhoods bright patches of fire. Demons rampaged through homes along the path back. I watched as legions of demons that had made their way inside the walls attacked people who stayed behind. Most of the lights outside had been shut off or destroyed, only the flames gave off light.

There were bodies spliced open on crucifixes outside on lawns, we watched as imps and demons supped upon their innards. The sight was a sad one. Many would not make it out alive, but they would afford many others safe passage into their new lives. This whole side of the world was about to go through a reset. We drove down the middle lane and passed countless atrocities on the other side. They all seemed to blur together as we flew by. The earth rumbled and the van bumped into the barrier. We swerved back into the middle and felt the tree awaken within the earth. Roots sprung up from the ground and plunged into demons that had invaded the territory. Vines pierced and snaked their way through the air, impaling demons that came nearby. I watched through the rearview mirror, hundreds of vines and roots destroying countless demons in their wake.

One particularly gigantic monster erupted from around a building to chase us, only to be upended, as a root the size of a boat crashed through the core of the demon and lifted him from the ground. It reminded me of what Terra had done to the demon before. It also made me question what I was doing, but now wasn't the time.

"Here we go," Maddy shouted as she drove out of the final barrier and into the fray.

Demons lined the road, and she barreled through them without hesitation. Loud pops, and splats littered the van. Guts and gore caked the windshield. The van's wipers fought hard to counter the violence. The tang of iron in the air from the blood seeped through the openings in the vehicle.

"Woo hoo," she cheered as she drove through them.

I heard Sloane retch in the back of the van. Rachel complained about how disgusting it all was.

"You're cleaning that up Sloane," Maddy yelled out. "Luckily there isn't any carpet in here to scrub." She laughed gleefully as the vomit sloshed to and fro.

I watched as she drove past the Sanctuary, the first place we stopped after entering Ouroboros. The insides had erupted and smoke billowed from inside.

All throughout the area The World Tree had posted demons up on spikes The corpses made for a frightening warning to other demons that might come this way. Sanctuary may be a true possibility here in the future. The van roared through the night as we crested back into the dark. The gate on the outside stood wide open and we flew past it. The ground crumbled away far behind us. True pandemonium reigned as the World Tree stretched back to life.

* * *

Minh grabbed the tree and began to shed the shell that was placed by Maurelius. His hands sunk into the wood and his skin became one with the tree. He could see the history in the tree and feel its emotions purer than ever. He felt the anger held deep within the roots, breathed in the eternal struggle between heaven and hell, maintained deep within the core. The branches swelled and the concrete ties buckled under the leverage.

Minh flexed his legs and the roots of the earth began to grow and creak under the weight of the concrete barriers. The structure inside began to crumble.

The souls who decided to stay realized then it was too late, the man on the television had spoken true, and they had not listened. Many tried leaping to their fates, meeting their end after a long fall. The floors that served as their shelter, crumbled to dust in front of them. Concrete shifted inwards and caused the floors to buckle and fall inward. The top of the building, the five-and-a-half-mile peak, plummeted towards earth.

The tree inside wriggled to be set free, throwing chunks of concrete for miles. The ground swelled as tree roots slaughtered the demons who made their way towards the base of the tree. He sent them back to the hell they had emerged from. The top of the tree shot new branches up through the falling skyscraper. Finally, free after being contained and restrained for years. Branches flexed and shook themselves awake.

The destruction was immense, the seven-hundred-mile radius where concrete fell was obliterated. Houses and societies were crushed as the building toppled. The spinning top of a building collapsed to the earth and encircled the mass of destruction. In the center, a gigantic tree stood proud and tall. The branches spread wide as they stretched to their full length. The water that was housed in the building flooded out and filled the concrete barrier to the top. What was once the most impressive building ever created, was now a massive lake with the Tree of Life as the center piece. It was a juxtaposition of beauty amongst devastation. Demons unable to climb the massive wall that was placed as the building fell. The survivors of the destruction who were lucky enough to be in the wall, lived on in their own way.

Minh became one with the Tree of Life and was its newfound guardian. Sharing his powers, while the Tree shared with him. Khadim had paved the way for this world. This was a strong start.

* * *

Maurelius watched from his home in the Outlands as the building he had poured his heart and soul into came to a crumbling end. The devastation leaving people dead for hundreds of miles. It was disgusting. This Constant was ruining everything. He threw his glass of liquor against the wall.

He would stop him if it took his entire being. The next human Constant after him, would just be killed on the spot to save all this trouble.

He had to contact Aibek, it was time that he helped end this affair with Khadim.

EPILOGUE

THE FALL OF Yggdrasil was just a stepping stone on the way to balancing the world. Ouroboros and Yggdrasil were no longer above others. It came tumbling down to clear a path for nature to take its place back. The fleeing humans would come to the real world and start a new path, free of the control of others.

Solace and Faul were dead. Though his physical body was gone, Minh lived on through the World Tree. I wanted to believe I wouldn't have to kill the others. I only knew one thing for certain, Maurelius needed to die. He must be wiped from existence; he was a plague on the world.

I only had a single regret...I never did get that shower.